Igor Savelyev was born in 1983 in Ufa (Bashkiria) where he still lives and works as a crime reporter for the local news agency. He has a degree in Philology from Ufa University. He made a name with his short novel *The Pale City* which was shortlisted for the Debut and the Belkin prizes in 2004 and published in France. *Mission to Mars* was published in Russian by Exmo in 2012. Many of his short stories have been translated into other languages. See also his "Modern-Day Pastoral" (in *Squaring the Circle*, Glas 2010) and "The Pale City" (in *Off the Beaten Track*, Glas 2011), both translated by Amanda Love Darragh.
Critics have noted his "finely chiseled style based on brilliant counterpoints like a virtuoso music piece."

Amanda Love Darragh is a translator of contemporary Russian literature, winner of the Rossica Translation Prize in 2009.

GLAS NEW RUSSIAN WRITING

contemporary Russian literature

in English translation

Volume 59

This is the ninth volume in
the Glas sub-series devoted
to young Russian authors:
winners and finalists of
the Debut Prize.
Glas acknowledges their
generous support in
publishing this book.

Igor Savelyev

MISSION TO MARS

a novel

Translated by Amanda Love Darragh

GLAS PUBLISHERS
tel: +7(495)441-9157
perova@glas.msk.su
www.glas.msk.su

DISTRIBUTION

In North America
Consortium Book Sales and Distribution
tel: 800-283-3572; fax: 800-351-5073
orderentry@perseusbooks.com
www.cbsd.com

In the UK
CENTRAL BOOKS
orders@centralbooks.com
www.centralbooks.com
Direct orders: INPRESS
tel: 0191 229 9555
customerservices@inpressbooks.co.uk
www.inpressbooks.co.uk

Within Russia
Jupiter-Impex
www.jupiterbooks.ru

Editors: Natasha Perova & Joanne Turnbull
Cover design by Igor Satanovsky
Camera-ready copy: Tatiana Shaposhnikova

ISBN 978-5-7172-0121-6

MISSION TO MARS
6

THE PEOPLE'S BOOK
183

MISSION TO MARS

CHAPTER 1

Putin stopped speaking. He held the camera in his hypnotic gaze for a few moments longer as snowflakes began to settle attractively on his black bureaucratic overcoat. A section of the Kremlin wall and some pine trees were visible behind him – bathed in floodlight, as though it were a landing site for alien spaceships.

Then came several panoramic shots of Moscow, at least the area around the Kremlin. Hardly any traffic. Just a few cars racing through the streets at top speed, red lights blurring, reinforcing the impression that this was a live broadcast taking place right now, at about two minutes to midnight.

There was a slight increase in animation around the table. The host, whom Pavel barely knew – a lad with big hands and strangely ruddy cheeks, probably due to frostbite – was untwisting the metal wire at the top of a bottle of cheap champagne. Far too enthusiastically. Despite his efforts to contain it, the cork flew out with a muted carbonate explosion before the girls even had time to squeal. Grimacing in despair, he tried to cover the neck of the bottle with his fingers.

"Problems with premature ejaculation?" joked Igor.

The others glanced at him scornfully, and not for the first time. It was only a matter of time before someone pushed the stupid bastard down a flight of stairs.

There was a distant detonation, accompanied by the faces of the Kremlin clocks on the TV screen. They looked as though they had been cut out of some kind of ancient, heavy cloth. When he was younger he had thought they were green, then dark blue; now they looked almost black.

They clinked glasses. The girls squealed. The boys grunted a kind of primitive cheer. The world outside erupted in a cannonade of fireworks and firecrackers, and Pavel remembered that he was supposed to make a wish. But he'd missed his chance.

After the national anthem, during which no one quite knew what to do with themselves, the TV camera cut to a shot of fireworks in the shape of 2007. This was greeted rapturously by the assembled company. Before, about ten years ago, the numbers used to loom straight out of the clock faces. Pavel could remember it quite clearly. They would grow slowly and inexorably closer, increasing in size with every strike. He had a particularly vivid memory of the year 1996 – dark blue figures with stark outlines, free from any cursive embellishment. "Like three sixes", his mother had said, and he had felt a sudden stab of fear.

But it was 2007 now, and everything was better.

Natasha had been gone for a month. (Better? Ha! Not exactly.) She couldn't fly directly, of course, so she had to go via Moscow. Her flight left so early it was still dark, and Pavel had lain in bed imagining his first day without her: his alarm clock would wake him at 8 a.m., he would reluctantly lower his warm feet onto the December floor, then he would remember that he'd been abandoned. In fact, the morning had begun in a different, painfully ordinary way. He overslept, for a start, and was woken by watery sunlight and a phone call from Sheremetyevo airport: it was Natasha, complaining that she'd forgotten to put any credit on her phone. She was worried that it might run out just when she needed it, and "none of the top-up points here work properly, and there's nowhere to change any money..." So Pavel had rushed about the kitchen, looking for something he could eat in twenty-five seconds flat. Then he had rushed into the city centre – standing up in a crowded minibus taxi, lurching with every gear change – to put a couple of hundred roubles' credit on Natasha's phone. He was worn out, there'd been no mournful lowering of feet to the floor, but it was still his first day without Natasha.

The day ended in the same absurdly non-tragic way it had begun. His friends had free tickets to some random gig, so he spent the evening surrounded by a chaotic, happy crowd at the entrance, inside the venue and then outside again. But it didn't change anything. In a plane crash, it doesn't make any difference how the bodies are scattered or what fragments of metal remain, covered in frozen condensation.

Pavel had been abandoned: the girl he loved had flown off to the States (Pittsburgh, to be precise) in order to continue her studies, to complete her industrial placement... She might find a job there. She might decide to stay.

Natasha specialized in a rather unusual field: she was an industrial furnace technologist. ("That's not very ladylike!" Pavel's mother had once said, pursing her lips.) The local Polytechnic was forever threatening to shut down her course, hobbling as it did from year to year, growing increasingly lame, from thirty students down to twenty. Illuminating conversations were held in the dean's office about which students to transfer and where to send them. Natasha smiled knowingly. Not her, no way: she was going to fight to the bitter end! Not because she was particularly fond of glass-works furnaces – ugly things that they were, foul smelling producers of light-bulbs. It was just typical of

Natasha. Once she set her mind to something, there was no stopping her.

First she became obsessed with the idea of transferring to the St Petersburg Mining Institute. Even if it meant losing a year, according to the recently adopted Bologna system, and a compulsory fourth year working in industry (she'd even started looking for a suitable factory). Whatever it took. Thus began a frenzy of visits to various deans and vice-chancellors, endless phone calls to the city on the Neva and so on. Eventually, she seemed to calm down a bit... And then she had another brainwave! She somehow discovered that transferring to the USA to finish her studies on a special grant program was not actually that difficult. There just weren't many people who knew about it. Natasha, with her stubborn tenacity, was more than capable of trawling the World Wide Web until she found out all she needed to know. It was quite simple, really. All she had to do was brush up on her English-language skills at night classes and be prepared to pay with high blood pressure for all the hours that she spent in the corridors of the US visa office.

Always reliable, Pavel was with her every step of the way. He never really believed that she was serious about leaving. She was so nonchalant about all the preparations. Meanwhile he shuffled alone through December with sore, chapped lips.

Evenings were the worst. Walking home beneath fairytale street lamps, scattering snow, Pavel would be overcome with despair the moment he walked through the door. He would sit in a stupor, rubbing his sore eyes and staring into space, before collapsing into bed early.

As soon as Natasha was settled in Pittsburgh she got into the habit of calling him on Skype, but their conversations were all somehow stilted, impassive. It was morning for her, whereas Pavel was still feverishly prostrate. He couldn't bring himself to feign enthusiasm before the toxic black porosity of the miniature microphone, but it wasn't only that – he felt that his stubborn, taciturn sulkiness was somehow justified. It contained a message to Natasha, an indirect reproach: "Look, I'm struggling here!" Natasha herself was clearly emotional, which might have been as much to do with problems she was having over there... But the fact was that they were in love, and the course of true (long-distance) love never did run smooth. They kept it up for about a quarter of an hour, Pavel heroically holding out for as long as he could, as he used to before, in different circumstances, then full of remorse the moment he clicked "End call".

Occasionally he would drag himself back out into the snowy courtyards, into shared minibus taxis full of strangers pressing up against one another, heads mournfully bowed. Like corpses hanging from the gallows. He visited his student friends – the few he had left. They had studied together at the local teacher training college, in the Social Studies and Humanities department, and their friends would often ask, not entirely seriously, "So what exactly do they teach you there?" Pavel had been hearing the same question for five years, and he still didn't know how to answer it. He was increasingly ashamed of his stupid, pointless education. The stiff, dark blue cover of his diploma might as well have been empty. All the important-looking stuff was there – the attractive watermarks inside the front cover, the heraldic crests, and so on, but it contained nothing of any value.

Being with his friends was as bad as being alone. Once you've exhausted every topic of conversation there's nothing left but to drink beer, the silence broken only by the noise of the fridge.

For example, Pavel would go round to Igor's apartment.

Igor – an ungainly, overweight and rather unattractive individual, with close-set eyes – was always delighted to see Pavel and greeted him with his usual over-the-top enthusiasm. If Igor's parents were at home he would furtively usher Pavel into his bedroom, bearing several bottles of imitation Guinness. The bottles were smooth and black. A bitter, hepatic elixir.

Igor liked to call himself a writer. Unfortunately, he genuinely seemed to believe that he was. He was apparently unable to move on from his obsession with the fantasy genre, and his short stories were frankly so dire that even the editor of the local youth magazine sometimes rejected them. Igor didn't take it personally, though, and continued to soil sheet after sheet of paper, ploughing relentlessly onwards like a blind bulldozer, crashing through every obstacle, unchecked by common sense. It had been a different matter when they were teenagers. When Igor passed him a folded note full of fantasy drivel in the middle of a tedious lesson at school, it was just a bit of a laugh. But now they were twenty-three, and one of them was taking it far too seriously, churning out the same old fantasy nonsense, the same old cyborgs. Nothing had changed (at least, not for the better).

"So, how's it going?" Igor asked earnestly, after they had downed their beers in conspiratorial silence. For crying out loud, what could possibly have happened in the course of two or three airless days?

Pavel left with the sour aftertaste of Guinness on his tongue, even more depressed than before, knowing that he would drag himself back from terminal despair over and over again.

Thus December drew to a close.

As New Year's Eve approached, when all the department stores and shopping malls had begun to heave and strain at the seams as was customary for the time of year, Pavel actually perked up a little. He announced that he wouldn't be celebrating at all, but would be going to bed early instead. This was perfectly understandable, of course. Oh, the solitary dignity of grief! But on the actual 31st of December, in a momentary lapse of judgment caused by excessive exposure to steam from the pans on the hob, Pavel allowed himself to be talked around. Danil was planning to spend the evening with some of his role-playing friends and had invited Igor to join him, so it was two against one and Pavel didn't have a lot of choice. He got ready to leave with as much enthusiasm as he could muster, which wasn't much at all, while his parents argued over the salads they were preparing and two alternating news images flashed on the TV screen: the indignant face of President Lukashenko of Belarus, and the Gazprom skyscraper in Moscow. Everything about the latter smacked of the early 1990s, from the evident lack of architectural inspiration to its industrial-looking concrete walls. A freak gladiolus. Pavel knew a bit about architecture. If things had been different... But they weren't. There was no point dwelling on it. The pressure compressed his brain, threatening to force out tears. Besides, it was nearly 8 p.m. and they had to get a move on, because Danil's bloody friends were expecting them.

Danil's bloody friends turned out to be an extremely mixed bunch. Half of them didn't even know one another. The girls stood awkwardly in the kitchen, unable to agree on which salads to make. The boys sat awkwardly in the living room, sipping their drinks in silence and pretending that they had never seen anything more interesting in their entire lives than the orgy of festivities currently being broadcast on TV. Igor was trying his hardest to get them all in the party mood, and in doing so was behaving like a complete buffoon. He seemed utterly oblivious to the fact that they were all glaring at him with undisguised hostility.

"I've got this one friend," he began. "Seriously, he's off his head! One year he spent New Year's Eve alone, and he had such a miserable time that when it was midnight he stood up on the windowsill... I guess he must have been standing on something else as well... Anyway, he stood up and just stuck his cock out of the top window. Like, 'Fuck you, New Year'!"

Silence. Everyone stubbornly scrutinized the explosion of artificial ringlets sported by the aging pop icon who was currently bawling her way through a song on TV.

"There was no one outside, though... I mean, it was midnight, right? So it's not like there was anyone to shock," added Igor, somewhat deflated.

Finally someone took pity on him. "He didn't lose it to frostbite, then?" remarked a red-haired guy wearing a signet ring.

The same guy ended up sitting next to Pavel at the table, so they started chatting. Turned out he worked on a building site. He declined Pavel's Putinka vodka in favor of the expensive stuff he'd brought with him. Pavel couldn't help noticing that his neighbour's nails were shining in a way that was somehow unnaturally healthy, like an onion glistening in vinaigrette. His neighbour saw him looking and confirmed that he'd been to a nail salon a couple of days previously to "tidy himself up a bit".

Downing a shot of Putinka and for some reason biting into a slice of fresh tomato – overwhelmingly tasteless after the vodka – Pavel gloomily reflected that this was a perfect sign of the times: a builder with a manicure. And it wasn't really even that surprising. A redistribution of roles was taking place, a new era was beginning, led not by techno-geeks, but by those engaged in physical labour. They were the ones with money, power and time, but most importantly, no psychological hang-ups. They could have whatever they wanted. They not only possessed the latest mobile phones and cutting-edge gadgets, becoming experts in computer technology and virtually fluent in English as a result, they also attended all the most sought-after concerts, private exhibitions, exclusive screenings and other fashionable events. A far cry from the "third-generation intelligentsia", from the son of a teacher who never went anywhere, never saw anything, didn't know anything and never would.

"Let's drink to the New Year in Moscow!" they cried at 2 a.m. "Come on, even though we've run out of champagne we can show our solidarity!"

They went outside to set off firecrackers and returned freezing but happy, their lungs full of fresh air and the smell of smoke. They broke up into small groups. Someone was already asleep on the sofa; someone else had positioned himself next to the cheap kitchen radio, thereby staking his claim to musical sovereignty.

"So, how's Natasha?" asked Igor. Although he wasn't exactly drunk, he was in even higher spirits than usual.

"Fine," replied Pavel. He mumbled something about Pittsburgh, the multi-racial community, Natasha's landlady, cockroaches.

"Is she coming back soon?"

There was no point answering such a stupid question, but Igor's eyes were already ablaze. He was doing what he loved best, making up stories.

"You know what... We should get them to kick her out of America! Why are you laughing? Seriously, they're always deporting people. Hey, I've got it! We could send her a letter with white powder inside! I mean anonymously, not actually from us. There'll be a police investigation, criminal charges and all that... As a foreigner there she won't stand a chance!"

"It would never get through our postal system," Danil remarked phlegmatically.

"No?" Igor didn't like it when other people interrupted his creative flow, but he refused to give in. "All right, what about this... Apparently they deported a couple of Pakistanis recently, for trying to get hold of some technical aircraft drawings, or something like that. Suspected terrorism... Perfect! We can stick some sketches in an envelope!"

He meant it, as well. This was what Pavel found the most worrying: Igor had absolutely no concept of the dividing line between real life and the endless kaleidoscope of fantasies that filled his head. Regarding himself as a modern-day Tolkien, he lived almost entirely in a world of his own invention. He had already started rushing about the apartment, wading through the aftermath of the party, asking the host about internet connection and a printer. Pavel felt a surge of indignation rising in him like water: he was a guest here (along with a random assortment of drunken weirdos), he was alone, he had been abandoned by the girl he loved (not even abandoned, merely pushed to one side) and now he was being ridiculed and laughed at... by Igor, of all people!

They carried on laughing at him as they sat in front of the computer, merrily scrolling through pages of search results, and then before he knew it Danil was printing out technical data from the Tupolev website and asking anxiously, "What about the Tu-104, will that do?"

"Stop it!" cried Pavel. "That's enough!"

"We're only trying to help!" Igor retorted cheerfully, but his smile faded.

"Just pack it in! Trying to help... How is this helping?

Natasha went to the States for a reason, and it was the right thing to do. She's building her career, making a new life for herself... Don't you get it? Why would she want to come back here? What's she going to do, sit around all day with me? With you lot? Who the hell do we think we are anyway? It's not an international hostage crisis!"

His friends froze, shocked into silence. Even Pavel was surprised by his own outburst.

"Okay, okay, take it easy," said Danil, ripping up the piece of paper he was holding.

"Pavel, seriously, we're sorry, okay?"

"You're doing my head in, both of you! Natasha this, Natasha that... Don't you think I feel bad enough already?"

After this little episode, it was clearly time to call it a night. In any case, it was already after 4 a.m. Pavel started getting ready to leave, ignoring his friends' attempts to persuade him to crash at Danil's apartment. He walked home alone through a city that was full of lights, still exploding with fireworks and festive salads, but already more than halfway to a hangover.

CHAPTER 2

"Volgograd! Number One for Volgograd!"

No one rushed forward. A variety of bags and suitcases, shapeless and anonymous in blue plastic wrapping and masking tape, were already making their third trip around the conveyor belt. Pavel and Natasha and the other passengers from their flight had been clutching pointlessly at the tags, checking the numbers against the counterfoils of their own baggage receipts, until they heard the announcement: it was all from Volgograd, apparently. Everyone stepped obediently away from the belt. So where was their bag? There wasn't a single passenger from Volgograd in the deserted arrivals hall, which had begun to resemble a warehouse with all the blue cellophane bundles lying around.

It was a couple of months before that depressing New Year's Eve, the beginning of October 2006. Natasha was visiting the US Embassy for the umpteenth time. Multicoloured papers, endless forms to fill in, limp fax printouts covered with fading text... Wasn't she tired of it all? This time, without making a big deal out of it and possibly because she felt she ought to, she had asked,

"Do you want to come with me?"

"To America?"

Natasha burst out laughing. To Moscow, of course, and no further. Two days. What else? Pavel agreed immediately. Not because he particularly wanted to go, and certainly not because he thought it would make any difference. In a month's time she would be on the other side of the world, somewhere beneath the soles of his feet, beneath the mantle and the core and whatever else was hidden deep inside the planet. For how long – a year? Maybe five? Or ten? He couldn't talk her out of it. He had no right to even try... But he couldn't simply let it happen. The idea of letting her go was too painful, even though he knew a couple of days in Moscow together wouldn't change her mind. A couple of mind-numbingly tedious days, spent travelling backwards and forwards on public transport, trudging through pedestrian underpasses, staying with friends of friends on the outskirts of the city... But he had to do something!

"Why don't you propose? Seriously! Ask her to marry you," Danil had suggested calmly the night before. Danil the calm, imperturbable, short and ridiculously long-haired role-playing fanatic. Master Danil. That was what all those role-playing losers called him, for some reason.

"Don't be stupid," Pavel said, waving the suggestion away.

But he went to Moscow anyway, and now here they were in Sheremetyevo airport, which was decidedly less glamorous than its palatial namesake, waiting over an hour for their luggage. Some of the ceiling lights were flickering on and off, as though they were taking photos of a crime scene. The passengers from their flight had dispersed: some were squatting down, others were wandering about aimlessly. Pavel was sick of the sight of them. A group of a dozen or so very tall young men with prominent kneecaps, all wearing long shorts, had settled down on one of the nearby carousels, like overgrown fledglings on a perch. They were members of a volleyball team from Moscow, returning from a tournament.

They had suffered more than anyone in the cramped aircraft and spent the entire flight swapping seats, standing up and begging the stewardess to let them into business class, which was half empty – a request that she politely yet firmly refused. The problem was that the seats were simply not big enough for them, and they hadn't managed to reserve the aisle seats, which had more legroom, because they'd been late getting to the airport.

"If we're flying long-distance they book us onto a bigger plane, with bigger seats," a colossal and very charming blond man explained to Natasha and Pavel. "But if the flight's less than two hours, we have to take a Tu-154. And the journey time from your city is exactly one hour and fifty minutes."

The young man tackled his in-flight meal with practised efficiency. It takes a certain skill to get the best out of all those little boxes, the plastic knives and miniature packets of butter.

He had swapped seats with someone who was sitting on

the aisle and squeezed in next to Pavel, saying, "You don't mind, do you?" Of course he didn't. It wasn't the worst flight ever, but it was still a pretty depressing experience. The time difference meant that they took off and landed at exactly the same time. Of course the aircraft wasn't a time machine, nor did it simply hang in mid-air... Though in terms of its position relative to the sun, effectively it did. They took off before dawn and landed before dawn, and there was something eerie about this early-morning gloom, with the cabin lights dimmed for most of the journey and the "No Smoking" sign glowing overhead. As if that wasn't bad enough, he was stuck with a talkative neighbour. Though at least you felt safe with someone like that next to you, Pavel thought with a smile, his shoulder pressing into a strong, muscular arm.

The volleyball player spent the entire flight either trying to sleep or standing up and looming over everyone else like an elephant. Shoelaces undone, stubble, fingernails the size of icons.

"I'm from Moldova, originally. The club basically bought me from there. Man, what a scandal that was! My parents and brothers are still there, and my friends. I try to go back whenever I get any time off... Which doesn't happen often, of course."

Pavel was preoccupied with his own thoughts. "Did you want to leave?" he asked after a short pause. His neighbour turned in his seat, which was no easy task, and gave him a look of baffled incomprehension. He didn't seem to understand the question.

"Not really, but the club gave me an apartment. It's all right, actually. I've just bought a Lexus too. On credit, of course, but still..."

The oversized birds began jumping off their conveyor belt perch as it suddenly jerked to life, heralding the appearance of the long-awaited bags and suitcases, frozen to their very core on their stratospheric journey.

Unfortunately, on one of her internet forums Natasha had read about a bus that went directly from Sheremetyevo to the US Embassy. They couldn't find even the vaguest confirmation of this, let alone any official information, but despite the fact that it was barely 7 a.m. Natasha was on one of her missions. Through the enormous windows they could see a whole row of minibus taxis, destined for the nearest metro station, but Natasha was having none of it. Leaving Pavel to look after their things, she rushed about the dreary, hungover airport in search of her mythical bus. The café attendants were yawning and there were people shaving in the toilets, like a scene from a Soviet film.

Eyes like headlights from lack of sleep, Pavel dragged their heavy bag round the airport, for the sake of something to do. He fixed his eyes on an advertisement taped to the wall in the corner, for the sake of somewhere to look.

Suddenly a spotty lad appeared out of nowhere and accosted him.

"Tbilisi?"

"What?"

"Are you going to Tbilisi? We're running a charter to Baku, and we can sort you out from there... Come on, let's go! We've only got a couple of places left."

"Sorry, what are you talking about?"

"If you've already bought a ticket to Tbilisi, I can help you get your money back without queuing..."

"Nutter," murmured Pavel, hoisting their bag onto his shoulder. Shrouded in blue plastic, it was heavy enough to contain a corpse.

Pavel and Natasha ended up taking a minibus taxi into Moscow after all, once all the seats were full, and a large part of the journey was spent stuck in the inevitable traffic jams. As the sky turned blue and the day grew warmer, the two of them slept cheek to cheek, as soundly as children.

It took about three hours to drop off their things and sort Natasha out at the embassy. Then Pavel dived into the metro with a sudden sense of freedom, not even knowing where to head first in the yawning chasm of time that lay before him. It wasn't the first occasion he'd found himself with time on his hands in Moscow, roaming for hours, for miles, through the city's covered walkways. His path always began in the centre, in Pushkin Square, where a bronze statue of the writer himself looked down on the skateboarders scattering the pigeons – even at this time of year, in the rain and mud. He remembered seeing a pirate's map in one of his favourite books, where the beginning of the path was marked with a skeleton. Was it *Treasure Island*?

Pavel stood at the back of his carriage on the metro, watching the carriage behind rocking from side to side like a wobbly tooth. He racked his brains, trying desperately to remember whether there were any books or CDs that he ought to buy while he had the chance. He couldn't think of any. Well then, he would just have to think. Here in Moscow, with nothing to do and no one to see, he couldn't avoid it any longer.

A ridiculously cheerful voice over the loudspeaker announced the names of the stations and reminded passengers that certain seats should be vacated for the elderly and passengers with children.

So, what should he do? He could always hope that Natasha was in the process of being refused her visa, but that was unlikely. Maybe he should go to the cathedral where Pushkin got married and light a candle, to make his wish come true. Ha! As if.

He had an extreme plan as a very last resort, which he tried to push to the very back of his mind... But he couldn't stand by and watch someone he loved just walk away. He had to clutch at every possible straw, even those he knew he shouldn't.

Just after they'd graduated, a friend of Pavel's from the same year had thrown a few belongings into a bag, waved goodbye to his parents, his friends and his country, and taken off. Quite literally. He had gone to the States too, but there no one was waiting for him at other end, just an aimless semi-legal, semi-vagrant life spent drifting from one dead-end job to another. Maybe tipping arctic shards of potato into burning fast-food oil was his dream? Unlikely. He probably didn't even have a dream. All he desired was this arctic freedom, with nothing and no one to hold him back. At least Pavel had a goal: to amputate his past, his whole life up to that point, to abandon everyone he knew, just to be with Her. To give up everything in pursuit of this goal, even if it meant washing cars or delivering pizza, forgetting his past and his own identity. Like a brainwashed slave.

A one-way ticket to Mars.

Could Pavel really do it?

Something caught his eye, an irritating distraction: two metal plaques, saying "roubles only" and "Actress Lyubov Orlova lived here" in English, had been fixed to the wall of the same house, side by side.

This was life taking revenge on him, because you should never betray your dream. He hadn't become who he'd wanted to; he'd been afraid of ambition, afraid of having a goal, and this was the result. He was no one. Natasha was building her future, but he... He was no one, and he had no right to hold her back.

It had all started at school, when he was about fifteen. Everything had come together: an innocent interest in architecture, fascination with the dusty tomes in the youth library, his talent for sketching... and the fact that his parents, surprisingly, seemed willing to support this prospective career choice. The Architecture department at the Polytechnic was so formidably serious that you could have been attending preparatory courses since early childhood and still find yourself studying round the clock, with varying degrees of success. So Pavel studied. Unfortunately, it was also formidably competitive.

He turned sixteen. Seventeen. During his final year at school, the laid-back attitude gave way to neurosis. His mother was panicking more and more, worrying incessantly, fussing and flapping: if he failed his entrance exams he'd have to do his national service. They couldn't afford a tutor to guarantee him a place at university. His father's feeble attempts to calm her down seemed only to make matters worse. Night after night Pavel, turning pale, was obliged to listen to them arguing through the wall.

The tension kept on mounting. It had to end somehow. Late one evening during the Christmas holidays, Pavel was walking home from a party. Flushed and high-spirited from the wine he'd been drinking, breathing in the ammoniac smell of the stars, he stepped out into the road, and...

The cars raced past, spraying him with filthy slush: Moscow had given birth to a sour October rain. At the intersection the flooded road changed colour, from green to red, and Pavel splashed deliberately across. His feet were already soaking. He didn't care. In ruined trainers, he crossed Red Square and turned onto the Embankment, following the curve in the Kremlin tower, its time-worn bricks.

He walked for a long, long time.

The illuminated facade of the Stalinist skyscraper on Kotelnicheskaya Embankment loomed conspicuously in the distance, despite the rain: Socialism's answer to Gaudí. It looked like an enormous stalactite, every wrinkle deliberately straightened out. But stalactites grow downwards, don't they? Pavel was like a bat, then, looking at it upside down. In fact he didn't need to look at it at all. He had sketched it in class until he knew it by heart.

But getting back to the accident... Happy and distracted, Pavel stepped out in front of a Jeep, whose ostentatious front bumper turned out to be stronger than his leg. It could have been a lot worse, though; his horrified parents were able to collect him later the same night, cheerful and contrite. The hospital reception area was full of ambulance medics and traffic officers wandering idly about, coarse and casual in their baggy canvas overalls.

Unfortunately, that wasn't the end of the matter. It was a complex fracture, involving splintered bone and yellow fluids – in short, a pain in the arse as well as the leg. He was off sick for three months altogether. No school, no studying. Pavel could, in theory, have coped. He could have pulled himself together, made up for lost time, overcome all the barriers and pursued his architectural dream. But it was impossible to make any sensible decisions while his mother was weeping and wailing. According to her it was a disaster, the end of the world! He wouldn't even finish high school, let alone get into university. Instead: army discipline, institutional bullying, Chechnya. But what if he became a teacher? The wheels were set in motion, and Pavel surrendered of his own free will. The only signs of his discontent were a sullen attitude and laboured breathing whenever he was forced to endure another quasi-medical procedure.

In the end, he finished school apathetically (no problems

with his graduation certificate, after all) and went to the Social Studies and Humanities department of the Teacher Training Institute, which was renowned for its lenient admission requirements and an acute lack of male students. Pavel subsequently wondered why he had been so swayed by his mother's laments, why he hadn't insisted on applying somewhere even marginally more prestigious and interesting where he could have specialized in something, anything, rather than nothing. He would have got in! But no. By stupidly playing it safe he'd ended up going along with the most idiotic, most worthless option available.

So Pavel's dream had been undermined, but only temporarily. He promised himself that much, at least. Limping in to join his new fellow students on the first of September, he tried to take it seriously but soon decided that at the end of the academic year (without a word to his parents) he would collect his documents and enroll in the Institute of Architecture. This cheered him up. With a sigh, he did his best to throw himself into the joys of turbulent student life.

During the spring term he realized that he might not be ready for it. That autumn he heard that the army enlistment office wouldn't allow him to defer again if he enrolled in a different establishment. So he decided to stay and finish his course at the Teacher Training Institute before doing another degree elsewhere, choosing to sacrifice five pointless years, throwing his "pound of flesh" to Fate. By this point, he already knew that he was lying to himself.

That was more or less how things turned out. No money, no strength to fight it, no longer seventeen years old. Apathetic and apprehensive, since the army had recently started actively enlisting graduates (who were not officially exempt), he gave into the persuasion of the ladies who ran the Social Studies and Humanities department and embarked on a postgraduate course, which was even more of a joke than his undergraduate course. Now his name was on a list. He was doing something useful, allegedly... Gradually he began to feel that he was living a life of no purpose. He had nothing to look back on. As for the future, what did it hold?

His immediate future held the courtyard of a skyscraper, strangely deserted. Metal-framed wire nets protruded from the first floor windows, presumably to catch rubbish thrown out of higher windows and the odd repentant Communist Party boss. (Ha!) A pipe from one of the air conditioning units fixed to the outside wall was dripping onto one of the memorial plaques, weeping inconsolably over an obscure hero of socialist labour. The name on the plaque meant nothing to Pavel.

We're all just brainwashed slaves.

He met up with Natasha later that afternoon. She was exhausted, her energy drained by the embassy. They trudged through muddy puddles that shimmered with multicoloured light, and went up to the third floor of an unremarkable glass building near the metro, lured by the "Café" sign over the door. The sign featured a cocktail in front of a radioactive lemon-yellow sunset, both skilfully woven from neon tubes. This had been Pavel's idea – to arrange something approaching a romantic evening before heading to the metro, making their way around the circle line, trekking out to the last station on one of the branch lines, catching a minibus and then tiptoeing through an unfamiliar apartment, whispering and bumping into each other.

But Natasha wasn't in the mood. She was listless, preoccupied.

"They took my fingerprints, can you believe it? I scrubbed the ink off as hard as I could."

To anyone watching she might have looked like a child, showing that she'd washed her hands before dinner.

It had been a good idea, coming here: a couple of salads, beer, a bit of meat. Music. A few sips, a few sighs, and Natasha started to relax.

"You know, when I was waiting in all those queues I started thinking... Am I doing the right thing? Do I really need to go?"

Pavel froze.

"But the fact is, I can't carry on like this either. I'm not talking about my course, or the lack of employment opportunities. I just can't live like this any more. It's like being stuck in a swamp. The same faces, the same routine – day in, day out. Do you know what I mean?"

Pavel looked into his beer. He had been stung by the word "swamp", and he wanted to make sure that she knew it.

"Please, don't take it personally." She took his hand.

Suddenly the lights went out, the radio stopped and the sound of worried voices rang out over a cacophony of jangling cutlery. For some reason the only continuing source of light was the fridge where the beer was kept, though its icy-looking shelves were virtually empty.

"Don't panic!" declared the barmaid. "It's been going off like this all day today. It's the casino downstairs. There's some kind of inspection going on, asset repossession or something, I don't know... Anyway, they're checking all the gambling machines, so..."

Chatting and joking, assuring customers that the lights would be back on soon, she went round setting candles out on the tables.

It was poignant, painful even, but Pavel couldn't help

being struck by the beauty of the moment, the way the candlelight fell so magically on Natasha's face. Maybe a romantic atmosphere wasn't such a good idea after all.

"I just don't want to end up like my mother, you know? We talked about it once... She had so many dreams! She wanted to become a cosmonaut like Valentina Tereshkova, and she was a certified skydiver. She showed me the documents to prove it. She was quite good at it too, apparently. And then look what happened."

"What happened?" Pavel echoed listlessly. It wasn't really a question.

"Nothing. That's the whole point. She got cold feet about learning to fly. She was too scared to do anything, nothing worked out for her and now all she does is complain about everything. Well, you know what she's like." Natasha had grown increasingly agitated as she delivered this speech. Now she looked down at her plate and fell silent.

It was true, he did know what she was like. Anna Mikhailovna, his would-be mother-in-law, was a deeply suffering woman. Her expression, her voice, the lines on her forehead were enough to tell you that her husband had left her with a child a long time ago, that she had trouble with her heart and that her music students ran amok during lessons. She would not turn and face them. Instead she would continue playing a polonaise despite the fact that no one was listening, and the reflection of her face would emerge from the polished surface of the piano, as pale as a drowned woman.

Pavel thought about the clumsy, overweight lapdog that Anna Mikhailovna doted on. It was brazenly cheating on its soft-hearted owner, dividing its time between two homes, running back and forth between Anna Mikhailovna and her next-door neighbours, no doubt imagining that the stupid humans had no idea. Once it forgot itself and ran up to Anna

Mikhailovna with one of the neighbour's slippers between its teeth.

Pavel clutched Natasha's hand.

"But if her life had turned out differently, you would never have been born."

"Oh, I would have been born, whatever happened!" Natasha declared with exaggerated bravura, eager to lighten the mood. She was smiling.

Just then the lights came back on.

He wished they hadn't.

CHAPTER 3

They were tightening a heavy-duty electrical cable around his neck, and it was impossible to tell which would ultimately prove stronger. He was clawing at the carpet with his nails. The marks were still there, by all accounts. Brutalized by panic and the cheap alcohol they'd been drinking, a gang of teenagers stood about the trashed apartment. The youngest and scrawniest of them, who had been assigned the role of lookout, was too scared even to look into the room.

How could Pavel possibly know these details? He opened his eyes. He had a headache and his eyelashes were encrusted with sleep. There were people lying about all over the place, bathed in the soft morning light, their breath sour and toxic from drinking. He didn't know how he knew. After all, it had happened a long way away – in Cheboksary – and a very long time ago. But this story somehow kept on spreading, turning into a shadow that followed Pavel's friend Danil wherever he went. Rumours had been doing the rounds of the Social Studies and Humanities department since the first week of the first year, or so it seemed.

Pavel stood up gingerly. He'd had too much to drink

and slept in his clothes, which felt disgusting to him now. They'd spent the night drinking in Danil's grandmother's apartment, which had three rooms and a weird perpendicular layout, like a crossword. Danil was living here alone while his grandmother was in hospital. It was strange the way two universes were able to share the same living space: heavy metal posters and piles of CDs, alongside countless jars of dusty medicinal herbs and other long-untouched keepsakes and relics.

Two massive wine glasses from the set in the sideboard stood on the table covered with CDs. Someone had obviously struggled to find a container for their contact lenses. A memorial toast to lost eyesight.

A week had passed since that arduous New Year's Eve when Pavel had allowed himself to be dragged out – as indeed he had now, to this pointless drinking session with the role-players Danil hung out with. What was he doing here? The whole week had been unbearably depressing. At least before he'd had lectures to take his mind off things; now there was nothing, not even a festive atmosphere. Pavel had spent the first few evenings of the year, traditionally so full of promise, sitting vacantly at home until it got late – and then he and Natasha would torment each other over the internet. Every night, shivering and sniffing, Pavel would sit there while Natasha ripped his soul out, leaving him as limp as a cloth puppet. Then another leaden day would begin.

And so it went on.

Tonight, for some reason, he'd come out drinking instead, on the pretext of celebrating Orthodox Christmas.

Things hadn't always been so bad, although they'd never been great. Danil was born in Cheboksary and had grown up there. His mother died when he was young. It wasn't exactly the classic wicked stepmother scenario (Pavel didn't know the details, because Danil never talked about it), but he soon went off the rails: low marks at school, wandering the streets, sniffing glue, hanging out with the wrong crowd. Things soon culminated in the intimidated youngster being initiated into "business". An older kid from the neighbouring courtyard had been going round boasting that he had two Sony PlayStations and his father was about to buy a Mercedes...

The brutality of the murder shocked Cheboksary.

In the event, Danil was a witness rather than an active participant; he was too frightened even to go into the room where they were torturing someone only a little older than himself (who didn't hand over his fortune after all; there was no fortune). Danil's age was relevant because he was too young to be subject to criminal responsibility. Not that it made any difference in the nightmare that followed – an endless series of police interrogations, court appearances, psychiatrists, persecution, press articles, registration with the police as a young offender, correctional school, nightmares, fear, panic, dread.

If it hadn't been for his grandmother, he would have gone out of his mind. His maternal grandmother had been a frontline scout, then a humble party functionary in a factory, and now she was a lively pensioner. She rushed about Cheboksary, brandished her medals, banged her fists, applied for guardianship and took her grandson away for ever.

Danil's new life in a new city started well. He worked hard at school, was quite good at sport, kept himself to himself and let his hair grow. Nevertheless, he came to understand that he'd be stained with the Cheboksary blood for the rest of his life. He had no choice but to accept it and retreat into himself. His details were automatically transferred to the local police station and would remain on record until he came of age. Everyone at school knew. All the lads from the courtyard knew, though they showed nothing more than guarded indifference. All the neighbours knew. Infamy permeated the air like a toxic gas, seeping through invisible pores from a different dimension. They didn't even want to let him enroll in the Teacher Training Institute at first, so his grandmother brandished her medals again, albeit with marginally less zeal than before. Danil had no intention of working as a teacher. He simply applied there because there was hardly any competition to get in, and when he left he took the first job that came along, which happened to be in the warehouse of a company that distributed household cleaning products. Stacking boxes was easy enough, the two-day shifts suited him – and that was all that mattered. This complete lack of ambition was a kind of elective deafness, a way of ignoring what people were saying and how they looked at him, a way of remaining calm and detached. In his own personal battle, this was his way of fighting back.

Right now he was asleep on the sofa, sandwiched between two other long-haired role-play fanatics. He'd managed to find a social group where no one was interested in who you really were, what your real name was, or what had happened in your past.

Ugh, it was so stuffy! Pavel went into the kitchen and opened the little top windows. The icy air flowed in, teasing the window frames.

He needed a cup of tea. A cup of tea, then home. Pavel picked up the first mug he saw and rinsed it out. On top of his hangover, he was in a really bad mood.

"Good morning! Though I'm not sure there's anything good about it," said Igor, coming into the kitchen with the imprint of whatever he'd used for a pillow branded on his face. "Whose idea was it to bring that balsam last night? What was it called? God, it was vile. Do you think it might have been laced with polonium? I feel like shit. Anyway, what are you doing up so early?"

"I just am," said Pavel. He sipped his strong tea despondently. "I need to get home. I've got something important to do."

"Housework?" Igor grinned.

"Maxim's coming. My second cousin."

"Ah, researching your family tree!"

"I want him to give me a job. He mentioned it last year, but I wasn't interested at the time. Idiot."

Under normal circumstances Pavel's abrupt, provocative tone might have made Igor wary, but his hangover had deprived him of all perspicacity.

"What kind of job?"

"I don't know yet. And believe it or not, I couldn't care less. It might be shoveling shit in a pigsty, for all I know!"

For some reason Pavel burst out laughing. Igor didn't get the joke. Pouring himself some tea, he committed the fatal error of embarking on a tedious lecture about the pitfalls of taking the first job that came along, just for the sake of it... Igor could usually be relied upon to start spouting pompous rhetoric on mornings like this.

Pavel exploded. "Enough's enough! We wasted all those years at college, now we're wasting even more on this postgrad farce. No motivation, no ambition, nothing! We can't even earn a decent salary. And we don't even care! We're happy to just sit around, waiting for some kind of 'calling' – only then might we deign to lift a finger."

Igor smirked, apparently not offended by the parody. Nevertheless, he couldn't let it go unanswered.

"So it's a decent salary you're after, is it? I can help you out with a loan if you're a bit short of cash, you know. You only have to ask."

"Oh yes, of course. I expect your parents keep you topped up regularly, don't they?" Pavel's tone was sarcastic. Everybody knew that Igor's family were well off.

"They do indeed." Igor smiled back at him. He was doing a heroic job of maintaining his composure.

Pavel could tell the path he'd chosen was a dead end and began to reverse clumsily, like an all-terrain vehicle stuck in the mud.

"It's not just about the money, anyway – I want to be doing something useful, to earn some respect! To earn my girlfriend's respect."

Pavel wanted to continue his angry tirade, but Igor's knowing smirk stopped him in his tracks. Igor didn't have the sense to keep his thoughts to himself.

"Ah, Natasha," he murmured.

"What do you mean by that?" snapped Pavel, his voice full of icy hatred.

"Nothing, nothing!"

The ironic expression on Igor's face was the final straw.

"You know what?" Pavel was choking with rage. He was going to say something stupid. Any minute now. "You like to think you're a great writer, don't you? Do you really think anyone actually wants to read what you write?"

Igor maintained a dignified silence, allowing the pause to hang in the air between them. There was something almost aristocratic about the way he was standing, and he really was displaying astonishing restraint. He was behaving more like a Soviet war hero than a hungover student. Igor allowed the pause to continue for a while before playing his trump card.

"I don't understand why you're telling me all this. It's

your problem, not mine! I've already got a job, in case you'd forgotten."

Already seething with indignation, Pavel was incensed by the smugness of this final remark. It was true. Igor worked freelance for one of the local newspapers, where he was paid a pittance and rarely bothered showing up, in true Soviet style. Laughing, he'd told them once about an editorial meeting where the editor, puffed up with a sense of his own importance, had instructed the student freelancers to research the various fields of national economy: one for each student. Igor got agrarian industry. His "research" had consisted of taking a black file, filling it with printouts of standard documents from the internet and placing it ceremoniously in the centre of the table. That was the last time he was ever assigned an article about agriculture (about which he knew nothing). But on the whole, everyone was happy. Although he had ended up at the editorial office completely by chance, it had all worked out perfectly. It kept his parents happy, for a start. He was studying for postgraduate qualifications and working at the same time – how very clever of him! The fact that he was living at their expense, well that was a temporary state of affairs, which just happened to be dragging on... and on...

Danil walked past half naked, his tangled hair hanging down his white back. Without acknowledging them, he went straight into the toilet and began throwing up noisily. It was so disgusting having the bathroom right next to the kitchen like that, with no sound-proofing. It was so disgusting, the way they lived. Igor gave Pavel a wry smile. Pavel suddenly felt even worse. He stood up, put his coat on and left.

The cold fused his nostrils together, and the pure white glare of the night's fresh snowfall hurt his eyes. Pavel took a few deep breaths, untangled his earphones and started walking. His portable CD player was a recent acquisition – it helped to while away the long minibus journeys home every evening, had an insatiable appetite for batteries and opened up to him a world of non-stop aural entertainment. Pavel had no particular musical preferences – he would listen to anything and everything, roaming the city with an eclectic assortment of rhythms in his head. Today, for example, it was the Beatles, whose vocal harmonies reminded him of the gypsies at the station.

A flurry of snow reached out towards him from the low roof of what looked like a kindergarten, or some kind of office. The local youth were playing hockey on the ice rink, every strike of the puck like the sound of breaking bone, and on the way to the station he passed not one but two elderly couples with skis slung over their shoulders, flushed from the frosty, pine-scented air, rosy-cheeked and happy. Pavel felt a strange pang of envy. Maybe I should take up a sport, he thought suddenly. Maybe a punishing exercise regime was a better way to reform himself ruthlessly, pushing his own limits until he could barely breathe. Training late into the night. Icy water at the crack of dawn. Pull yourself together, man!

Maxim was waiting for him, stuffing his face with salads. Tall and going on thirty, he was laughing raucously. He was a distant relative, his connection with Pavel's family dating back to the time, many years ago, when he'd come from the depths of the provinces to go to university in the city and had stayed with them for quite some time. Pavel must have been about twelve at the time, maybe a little older. Things were so different back then. Maxim had been a skinny teenager, with the shadowy beginnings of a moustache, and Pavel could remember how proud he'd been of his provincial school leaving certificate. They were printed in old-fashioned faded brown tones back then, and the round stamp looked as though the ink-pad had been saturated with whatever liquid they could find.

"You came to me at just the right time, as it happens. Another two weeks and I might not have been able to help, but right now I'm looking for an assistant. Our team is growing. There are only two of us in the office at the moment, but soon we'll be three."

"What office?"

Maxim laughed. He looked pretty pleased with himself. It must have been the festive mood, or the amount of food he'd eaten. Or maybe he went cross-country skiing every morning.

"Hats off to you, cousin – you don't even know where you're going to be working, do you? The regional office of ARTavia. Have you ever heard of the company?"

Five minutes of shame: he knew nothing, he'd never heard of anything.

"Well, I don't suppose there's any reason you should have," said Maxim, suddenly swapping his raucous laughter for a more serious tone of voice. "We don't advertise, and we're not interested in increasing our passenger numbers. In any case, we don't have any obvious selling points. Our prices are high, and we don't offer discounts. We work specifically with individual VIP clients, people who can afford us, if you know what I mean."

Pavel thought he did. With a sinking feeling he imagined having to get trussed up in a suit and suffocate himself with ties on a daily basis. But then, what difference did it make?

"We only fly to Moscow and back. Why bother flying anywhere else? That's the only domestic route anyone's interested in and we don't have a licence to fly abroad, but that's another story. Head office supply us with aircraft that have been refitted throughout in business class. Imagine that!"

Pavel nodded apathetically, mildly surprised by the

childish pride with which Maxim shared this unremarkable information. Maxim was looking at him with a conspiratorial expression. "I know what you want to ask me," he said.

Pavel had no idea what he meant.

"About the salary. Don't worry, I'm not expecting you to work for free... Your first month will be performance based, though. Because it's a trial period, obviously. You okay with that?"

"Yes, of course," said Pavel. Yes, of course, he thought. Not that he cared.

At this point Maxim – who was still stirring a pearlescent lump of sugar into one of their best china cups – stood up, shook Pavel's hand firmly and began bellowing compliments at his mother, which continued through the hall and onto the landing outside the apartment. Pavel wished he would just hurry up and leave. As soon as decorum permitted, he went back into the apartment and leaned his forehead against the cool glass of the window. The day was aging magnificently: the shadows were lengthening, and everything was bathed in gold. A young couple walked past carrying a baby. Spread-eagled in a padded snowsuit, it looked like a starfish.

What time was it in Pittsburgh? Was Natasha asleep, or was she waiting for him? Had she tried to get hold of him earlier, when he'd been sleeping off the vodka at Danil's place? Everything was merging together. He couldn't face the thought of moving, setting up Skype, another silent conversation, trying to overcome the remains of his hangover.

It was all too much.

CHAPTER 4

Ivan Korogodin raised the nose of the aircraft too aggressively, exceeding the critical angle of attack.

Ivan Korogodin was the pilot of the Tu-154 aircraft that crashed in the steppes just outside Donetsk, in eastern Ukraine, on 22 August 2006. The passengers on board were returning from their holidays in Anapa, on the Black Sea coast.

Local residents recalled hearing bursts of thunder out of the blue, reminiscent of the intense bombardments of 1941. They also recalled the scorching heat, its desolate calm no doubt resounding with the chirping of grasshoppers.

The city was a faded version of itself, as far as Pavel was concerned. While he spent the blinding month of January trudging about ferociously and indiscriminately, like a bison in a forest, the newspapers were full of endless articles about the tragedy that had taken place in Donetsk back in August. The reason for this renewed flurry of interest was that the Interstate Aviation Committee had begun to publish the results of the investigation. A number of different theories had been put forward: a lightning strike, for example, allegedly the first occurrence in contemporary civil aviation (or possibly the first significant case of divine intervention in the modern era).

The IAC reported that in attempting to rise above the storm front the aircraft had reached an extreme altitude of 11,900m. The temperature at that height was unusually warm that day: -36°C as opposed to -55°C. The air was rarefied and the engines were struggling to cope with the weather conditions, as were local residents on the ground below.

The articles went on to say that Ivan Korogodin had disabled the autopilot, thereby deliberately entering into manual flight mode. The angles of attack and pitch (the position of the aircraft relative to the flow of air) exceeded the values necessary for the angle of attack limiter and the overload alarm to kick in.

The overload alarm was precisely what had been

pounding in Natasha's sleep-deprived head at the time. She had spent the entire summer taking exams, as well as printing out an ever-growing pile of application forms for American universities. The forms were so complicated, the writing so small, that the printouts were not always legible.

According to the charts, the aircraft started to malfunction. It ascended 833m in just ten seconds, which was quicker than the subsequent descent. "This phenomenon is known as a pick up," explained the newspaper expert. "It is a constructive peculiarity of the Tu-154: at a certain angle of attack, the airflow around the wing is disturbed with the result that the aircraft is propelled upwards." The aircraft ascended almost vertically, then entered stall mode and fell into a flat spin, crashing 45km outside Donetsk.

Natasha was exhausted from trying to navigate her way through the application forms. She was in a bad mood. She sent Pavel off to find an English-Russian dictionary of legal terminology, which was not available for love or money.

Whilst seeking to avoid areas of storm activity and turbulence, the crew allowed the aircraft to enter pitch oscillations exceeding the operational range of angles of attack. Lack of control over the flight speed of the aircraft and failure to follow guidelines on preventing the aircraft entering stall mode, coupled with unsatisfactory coordination amongst the crew, led to...

Basically it crashed, and Natasha left shortly afterwards.

Pavel read all about it during the first week at his new job. Relevant newspaper articles had been cut out and collected in a red file, which had apparently been left by the previous occupants of the office.

Reading the articles took him back to the first falling leaf, rare and golden, back to the turning point between summer and autumn, and he had an unpleasant recollection of hearing two similar reactions to the catastrophe. The first he had struggled to hear at all because the radio reception on his portable CD player, unreliable at the best of times, kept cutting in and out as he made his way through the labyrinths of the city centre in a minibus taxi. The radio station was broadcasting an interview with a fashionable city DJ, who clearly loved the sound of his own voice. Pavel caught only fragments: "Plane crash... inspired me... I felt rather sad for them."

Rather sad for them.

The second incident concerned Igor, who had come up with an extraordinary version of events. He'd seen an amateur video clip taken on a mobile phone (which had been bought from some youths in the nearby village of Sukha Balka and retransmitted by the central TV channel), and it had obviously made quite an impression on him. The clip was highly pixelated, and there wasn't much to see – some frantic running, an explosion in the distance. Igor had been struck by the coincidence, by the fact that a local boy just happened to be walking in that particular field with his mobile phone when all of a sudden, from out of the sky...

The worst thing about Igor's story was the fact that there was something in it – a suggestion, a feeling, a nuance. An aircraft crashes in the middle of nowhere and a swarm of people arrive – journalists, all kinds of experts. Devastated, the primitive locals come together in the evenings, gathering quietly around a paraffin stove (or the closest equivalent). These stunned, silent evenings held for Igor a kind of unexpected integrity.

Pavel criticized the story all the more vehemently for this reason. (Because of this, Igor never did get round to writing it down.)

According to Igor, these discussions amongst the

villagers gave rise to an idea: the transport minister himself was there, spearheading the investigation, and they needed a road to the village. So they approached him with a petition. On hearing it, his response was, "But I'm a Russian minister, and this is Ukraine..."

The End. More or less. Bravo! What a load of bollocks.

That's what he was like: Igor Aleksandrovich, the Great Writer.

"Why are we collecting all these?" Pavel asked in surprise, as he flicked through the recent press articles in the red file. The IAC reports, as always, were abundantly diluted with editorial input: techniques to overcome the fear of flying, how to breathe in the event of a panic attack, the correct way to put on an oxygen mask, and so on.

"It's part of our job," Maxim replied enigmatically.

They had spent the last few days at ARTavia's regional headquarters, which was situated on the fourth floor of a business centre, a dull, square box at the far end of the city's main street. As if to demonstrate its hi-tech credentials, the building was covered entirely with unnaturally dark blue glass. Whenever the sun was shining, car drivers were virtually blinded by the intense, dark blue reflections. You didn't have to be an architect to know that this ostentatious glass and chrome facade concealed cost-cutting and shoddy workmanship. Pavel had an ominous feeling that the windows wouldn't open, the air conditioning wouldn't work properly and the whole place would stink of plastic.

The reality was only marginally better.

Pavel hadn't spent much time with Maxim since the two of them had sat together in the semi-darkness one evening all those years ago, and Maxim had shown Pavel his secret: a strange pink mark on his wrist.

"What's that?" asked the adolescent Pavel, alarmed.

"Proof that I'm one of the lads," Maxim whispered proudly. He went on to explain that in their village it was the way they initiated new recruits into the gang, stubbing a cigarette out on their arm to see if they would scream or cry. "When they're about your age," added Maxim, and little Pavel wondered in consternation whether or not he would have screamed.

Now he was wondering whether or not Maxim still had the mark, and he couldn't stop glancing sideways at both of his wrists (he couldn't remember which one it was) to try and see beneath the impeccably tailored cuffs.

Maxim had changed a lot. Natasha would probably follow someone like him to the ends of the earth. He exuded success and purposefulness. Every morning he would stand in front of his desk like the captain of an ocean liner, eyes narrowed, strong teeth in an impeccable smile.

They were the team: Maxim, Pavel and Elya the secretary, who was unsurprisingly blonde. Rather incongruously, Elya was taking a correspondence course at the Institute of Agriculture (though she was specializing in some aspect of economics). She was harmless enough and spent most of the day surfing the internet. One day Elya was out of the office because she had an exam and Pavel needed some documents urgently, so he logged in to her computer and inadvertently found himself in one of the online chatrooms that she frequented. It was one of those anonymous, poorly formatted sites designed for the younger generation to discuss the things that bothered them, and it appeared that his colleague's user name was Enter-Elya. Interesting, if not particularly original. It was a pity he hadn't told Maxim about it, as he would have enjoyed making some crude joke about entering Elya.

The office itself was just like any other office. Pavel

noticed a piece of paper taped to the wall above Maxim's chair. It was a form filled out in careless medical scrawl, with a violet stamp and a kind of printed emblem. Pavel recognized the universal symbol for radiation. Peering at it more closely, he noticed that the text was in Ukrainian.

"Yes, I went to Chernobyl. Well, to Prypiat," said Maxim, by way of explanation. His voice contained a hint of pride. "This summer. Bloody expensive... But I went on a two-day trip, and it was great!"

"Ooh, isn't it dangerous?" exclaimed Elya, widening her eyes in horror.

"Dangerous? You mean the radiation? That's all bollocks. At least, there aren't any side-effects from just two days. And you wouldn't believe how many tourists there are, particularly from Europe. Our guide said that one of the Germans called it Disneyhell."

"They have guides?" Pavel imagined coach-loads of tourists being herded around.

"Yeah, it's all organized groups... You know what it reminded me of? Cuba. The same way Cuba's a kind of open-air museum for Buicks and Cadillacs, the whole area round Chernobyl is like a museum too. I spent a day just walking around, wandering in and out of apartment blocks, taking it all in, and at some point I realized that I'd seen it all before – in photos. All those little gas masks on the floor of the kindergarten, you're not even allowed to breathe over them, can you imagine that? They've kept everything exactly as it was, the way it was abandoned. And because no one lives there any more, it's starting to look really dilapidated. I mean, some of the buildings, it's hard to believe they're still standing. They were all built at the same time as our apartment blocks, right? They even look the same. So you've got maybe three or four memorable images and herds of people tiptoeing around them, trying desperately not to touch the damn gas masks. It was a disaster area, now it's a photo opportunity!" Maxim was delighted by his new-found wisdom.

"The mountain that gave birth to a mouse," murmured Pavel, wondering how much of Maxim's account was true and how much was exaggerated for effect. He also wondered whether he would be capable of walking amongst children's gas masks without shuddering. Probably. After the hundredth conceptual photo-session, artfully arranged by some fashionable but jaded genius, he too felt "rather sad for them". And that was all.

There was definitely some kind of connection, faint but nevertheless perceptible. Prior to encountering the red file Pavel had never even noticed the way the press seemed to relish plane crashes, the way they shamelessly borrowed words and phrases from aviation terminology, combining them with graphic descriptions of the final moments of the fatal flight. All of it devoured by the passenger in the departure lounge, reading his newspaper (whilst clutching his boarding pass and listening out for his flight to be called), feeling his blood run cold – like a visitor to Chernobyl, like an addict, wanting more, more!

Pavel's desire to immerse himself completely like a Stakhanovite, blocking out memories, thoughts and feelings, manifested itself in an unprecedented display of enthusiasm during his first week at work. He even made a couple of suggestions to his boss. For example, he remembered Maxim saying that their aircraft were refitted throughout in business class. He also remembered the poor volleyball players, who couldn't fit into their seats and had to stand in the aisle with their heads bowed, like fish hung up to smoke. Why not offer them the spacious seats of ARTavia instead? They could become the airline of choice for all volleyball teams, sign some kind of exclusive deal with the clubs – and if they were signing up all the players in a team, then they'd probably be able to offer some sort of discount, wouldn't they?

"No," said Maxim, after listening to Pavel's impassioned proposal with a detached, vaguely sympathetic look on his face. "We don't give discounts. Moscow wouldn't let us, even if we wanted to, and the clubs won't be interested anyway. Take my word for it. Our tickets are twice, almost three times more expensive than our competitors' on the same route, and they can't afford it. Their sponsors would just say it was unnecessary expenditure, end of story. They're all clamping down at the moment."

"Three times more expensive? Who's going to want to fly with us at that price?"

"Oh, people do," Maxim assured him, drawing the words out for effect. "We're not completely full, of course, but we're not far off. Virtually all the wealthiest people in the city fly with us."

Pavel felt as though he were struggling at the bottom of an economics class. The teacher, meanwhile, was relishing his role.

"This is what it's all about," declared Maxim, brandishing the red file. "These articles. I mean all the air disasters, the endless emergency landings. This is how bad it's got... I've been flying all my life, but this autumn I flew to Egypt and as I sat there I could feel every one of those ten thousand metres beneath my arse. I couldn't even chew my food properly. Our country's so big that anyone who's serious about doing business has to fly, but many are afraid to, and in return for security, for a complete and absolute guarantee of safety, they're prepared to pay not just three but ten times more. Do you know what I'm saying?"

"Not really," admitted Pavel. Although it wasn't

beyond the realms of possibility, he thought to himself. If you had brand new aircraft, and an extremely experienced crew... But, but... "But what do you mean by an 'absolute guarantee'?"

"I mean our clients know that our aircraft won't crash. Ever. Not under any circumstances," said Maxim, carefully enunciating every word.

"What are you talking about? How can anyone possibly give that kind of guarantee? What if there's... I don't know... a hurricane, or something?"

"Come on, don't get so worked up about it," replied Maxim, dismissing Pavel's questions with barely concealed derision. He'd already dropped the edifying tone and Sovinformburo attitude. "You'll understand it all soon enough. For the time being, just watch how Elya and I do things... What do you say, Elya my dear? Shall we give the boy a master class?" Maxim gave a crude laugh.

In the event, there were no master classes. Sometimes there were clients, middle-aged men, who sometimes brought their wives. Maxim fawned over them. The men filled out forms, rejecting the pen that was offered them, and in return they were given plastic membership cards. You couldn't buy a ticket here without one, which was no doubt supposed to evoke the exclusivity of a British gentlemen's club. Pavel looked on with mild amusement. These men were readily handing over quite significant sums of money, sometimes in cash. He learned that bundles of 500-rouble notes turned deathly pink when cut open, like an onion. Sometimes there were 5,000-rouble notes, too, which Pavel had never seen before. Elya artlessly labeled them the "colour of shit".

Pavel was exhausted at the end of every day, despite the novelty of it all. As he trudged wearily home beneath stooping street lamps the wind began to pick up and the street lamps gently shook their heads in the fiery shafts of the blizzard, as though they were trying to tell him something. His mobile phone rang.

"Where have you been?" asked Igor, being deliberately obtuse.

"I've been busy at work," Pavel answered icily. His injured feelings had coalesced into a strange ball, as though he were upset not only with Igor, but also with himself... And maybe Natasha?

"Do you want to come over to my place? We could have a few beers?" Igor's desperation was pitiful.

"Not today. I'm too tired," said Pavel. He rang off without saying goodbye.

An injured Volga was snarling in the courtyard of his apartment block, and he had to help haul it out, getting covered with wet snow. That was nothing, though. Dragging himself out of his own rut was an altogether more daunting prospect.

CHAPTER 5

How did they meet? Pavel loved thinking about the hours they'd first spent together, despite the dank autumn drizzle that had soaked them to the skin, despite the pointless stupidity of the circumstances.

Pavel was no activist. Even at school he had objected strenuously whenever they'd tried to assign him extra-curricular roles, to entrust him with the wall newspaper (expecting him to work some nocturnal magic with poster nibs and ink), or to coerce him into joining clubs along with the other reluctant, intimidated students. But in a faculty dominated by girls, he found that resistance was futile. Pavel had no choice but to step forward, and so he did. He was stunned to hear himself speaking at the Student Spring Festival and barely recognized his own voice, but the event where he'd met Natasha was a student rally that the dean had insisted they all attend, which took place during the autumn of his final year.

Young people bearing banners stood around getting wet in the square, which was inky black from the rain. It took a while for it to sink in that the assembled youth were expected to emulate the "student construction detachments" of the 1950s, which were experiencing a peculiar local renaissance. Since in reality such detachments did not exist (at least, not yet), anyone present could join in. The assembled students flapped their wet flags furiously, like something out of a Soviet propaganda film. Hip flasks were passed around, smiles were exchanged. They waited and waited, though no one seemed to know what they were waiting for. The speaker, a local actor who appeared to be tormented by obscure passions, was also flagging – he'd already told them three times that Putin had used his student earnings to buy his first Zaporozhets car. (As though there had been a second.)

Pavel couldn't remember how he'd first started speaking to Natasha, a pretty activist from the Polytechnic whose hair was plastered to her face, because she categorically refused to cover her head with a carrier bag like the other girls. Half an hour later they were happily knocking back a dangerously alcoholic cocktail from a plastic bottle that someone held out to them; an hour later they were shouting fanatically at the top of their lungs. By now the crowd were chanting various slogans in unison: "The energy of youth, working for the region!" and "Our region, forever young!"

When the local governor eventually took the stage to the opening bars of the soundtrack from *Star Wars*, Pavel and Natasha burst out laughing and collapsed into each other's arms. When it was all over they carried on drinking and wandering the city, initially with a group of fellow students then just the two of them.

After that, Pavel came down with a cold. When Natasha called and they met again (and his heart stood still with anticipation), he was surprised by her light-brown hair. The rain had made it look almost black.

Two years later here he was, caught up in his memories, wading through snowdrifts on the outskirts of the city. It was primarily an area of privately owned houses with grey gardens, their branches inter-linked like horns, and in the summer it was an aromatic sea of green, so alive with buzzing insects that you couldn't help bumping into these chitinous creatures as you stepped out of the sweltering bus.

Natasha had been in the States for some time, but Pavel still remembered the way to her apartment block, a five-storey building that resembled a cruise ship cast adrift. He had promised her mother that he would be there by 2 p.m. and it looked as though he was going to be more or less on time.

Natasha had asked him to go round. It was all her fault. Even though she already knew that she was going to the States (at least, so she hoped), she had decided to start redecorating her bedroom that summer. The cosy apartment, housed in a building surrounded by a sea of apple trees and ramshackle sheds, was inhabited exclusively by women, so naturally Pavel ended up helping. The job itself was done by a taciturn female decorator, but Pavel moved the tables, the sofas and the cupboards, while Natasha's mother reverentially ladled him out a second helping of *borshch*. Natasha had been absolutely obsessed with choosing the right wallpaper. They had traipsed around the shops until they were completely exhausted, Natasha calling her mother every minute, taking photos of samples on her phone so she could send them by SMS. Then her mother couldn't work out how to open the messages, and tempers began to fray.

Then autumn arrived and it was all in vain. The occupant of the room no longer cared about the wallpaper, which, incidentally, had been hung rather well (the ceiling certainly could not have been scraped more thoroughly). Now preoccupied with air travel, long-distance correspondence and her ongoing battle with the US State Department, she had lost all interest in the unfinished redecoration project. She seemed perfectly happy to sleep in a room with furniture and boxes all over the place, like a railway station. That was where they said their goodbyes. Parting was painful enough as it was, but the splashes of paint on the cupboards somehow made it three times worse. The room was in complete disarray. Natasha's belongings were scattered all over the place, giving the impression that she was abandoning a sinking ship and those who remained were about to be submerged in sorrowful, icy water.

Anna Mikhailovna was choking on her sorrow. Weak, prone to hypochondria, incongruous and absurd, she was now alone in the silence of the apartment, with only the monotonous ticking of the kitchen clock for company. It was understandable that this visual reminder of the departure of her only daughter was more than she could bear. Who would put the cupboards back where they belonged? Natasha had asked Pavel, of course. So now he was walking through the park, which he remembered from his own childhood.

The park was deserted. He passed the enormous stone memorial to the fighters for Soviet power, which was always cold despite its eternal flame and the cats that skulked eternally around it.

When Pavel was a boy, in the early 1990s, this flame

had been extinguished. The burner fell overwhelmingly silent and turned a hideous, nondescript colour. Half of the bronze letters that had spelled out the names of fallen warriors were removed by vandals and Pavel had been overcome with... not fear, exactly – of course it wasn't fear, but a nagging feeling that in the future no one would ever know the exact names and surnames of the people buried here. They were so meaningless, so irrelevant, that they had been erased by the sands of time and lost forever. Now, though, new bronze letters sparkled amongst the old ones and Pavel smiled at his own childish naivety: had it really not occurred to him that they might be recorded in some archive or filing cabinet?

Anna Mikhailovna hadn't changed. She was still wearing the same old-fashioned glasses, which reminded him of a certain Soviet actress from the 1960s.

"I hope I'm not putting you to too much trouble, Pavel dear," she fussed.

"Not at all. I don't work at weekends."

"Of course not, it's only schools that work on Saturdays. I'm not working today, though, it's my library day!"

Pavel was reminded of the times he'd been unable to put off visiting the library as a student. Sitting with his pile of books, he had been so distracted by the disturbing pot plants that he found it impossible to concentrate. An enormous, ancient cactus propped up by an even more ancient ruler. Dusty old succulents. Ruined pots.

The memory was abhorrently precise because the state of the apartment itself reminded him of the library. When her daughter left, Anna Mikhailovna had simply given up. Certainly as far as the housework was concerned. There was a damp, neglected feel about the place, and you kept expecting to walk face first into a spider's web in the bathroom.

"Pavel, will you have some soup? I've made *rassolnik*!"

He was about to decline automatically, but his stomach started rumbling and he realized belatedly (after he'd already said yes) that she'd probably made it especially for him. He couldn't bear the thought of offending her, and besides, the *rassolnik* was actually pretty good.

"How's Natasha?" asked Anna Mikhailovna, watching with approval as her would-be son-in-law ate his soup. She asked as though he'd come straight from Pittsburgh. His surprise showed on his face, and she noticed.

"She says you talk over the internet, like on the telephone. I don't really understand it all."

Pavel stirred *smetana* into his bowl of soup, creating a kind of murky suspension, and didn't know how to respond. Things hadn't been great between him and Natasha lately. They couldn't even have a normal conversation because she was so oversensitive, even when she was in a good mood. She seemed to be on edge the whole time. And that wasn't all... Yesterday she'd suggested they try Skype sex.

"What?" Pavel was (almost) speechless.

"You know... We can talk, and you can, you know... touch yourself, and I can too..."

When her voice became awkward like this with embarrassment and she spoke secret words as though they were a foreign language, it usually turned him on. (He never knew how to sound right in bed either.) But not this time. He wasn't a prude, but for some reason he found the idea a sacrilege, although he didn't even fully understand the reason for his own indignation. Was it because it seemed to somehow demean his current state of miserable celibacy? (He knew this was stupid, of course.) Whatever the reason for it he couldn't hide his puritanical astonishment, although he did try. Natasha had even shed a few tears.

And now her mother was asking him about Skype!

It was unbearable. He really ought to get on with those cupboards.

Very carefully and with great effort they moved everything back into place, steadying the feet of the furniture with folded newspaper that had previously been used to wipe off smears of fresh putty. They took particular care not to break the feet themselves, because they were already cracked. The lapdog rushed about ecstatically, interfering and generally getting in the way.

Anna Mikhailovna tried to help but was as much of a hindrance as the lapdog, picking things up the wrong way when it was obvious that they were too heavy for her, and so on. Pavel secretly found it impossible to believe that this shortsighted old woman, with her ludicrous upside-down glasses, had ever jumped out of a plane with a parachute or dreamed of becoming a cosmonaut. What had become of those dreams? It just goes to show, life sometimes has other plans for us.

On the way there Pavel had been feeling bad about upsetting Natasha, but now his feelings were rising in revolt. She was so selfish! Trampling all over people... It was fine for her to do it to him (in fact, it wasn't at all), but how could she abandon her own mother, leaving her all alone and confused? Fair play to her for pursuing her studies, but it seemed to be at the expense of all human decency.

He couldn't tell whether or not Anna Mikhailovna was genuinely pleased to see him. She was certainly treating him like a welcome guest and showing an interest in his life. "You've got a new job, I hear?" she asked. "Natasha mentioned it."

"Yes," Pavel answered readily. "Yes..."

He proceeded to tell her a bit about the company and was amused to acknowledge within himself a childish desire to embellish the truth, to exaggerate his role in "the aviation business". So that she would pass it on to Her.

He and Natasha hadn't been together long when she began to show increasing interest in his lack of employment, given that he was already in his final year. Natasha herself was always doing something besides studying, whether it was temping in an advertising agency or standing in a shopping centre handing out flyers. Her phone never stopped ringing, and she always seemed to be late for something. In the end Natasha had to virtually drag Pavel to his first job, which turned out to be equally pointless. It was with some friends of hers, who had a vacancy for a junior manager. She wouldn't stop going on about it. On and on and on.

He stuck it out for several months, turning up as required, drifting through the days, doing very little and getting paid a pittance. Then he had to leave. His parents were getting agitated, putting pressure on him, wearing him down. They pointed out that it was his final year, he had exams coming up and his postgraduate course to apply for. "You haven't got time for a job," they said, and Pavel wasn't about to argue. Neither was Natasha; she was already obsessed with the idea of transferring to another institution to finish her studies and could think of nothing else.

Pavel hadn't really worked since then, for one reason and another: Natasha leaving, a bit of casual income... Then there was the endless autumnal melancholy, which yielded only to winter melancholy.

Darkness had fallen. There was the faint smell of dust, warmed by the lamp. The cupboards had been moved. So it was probably time to put on his boots, indelibly stained with February snow, and head off.

Just at that moment, Anna Mikhailovna thought of

something she wanted to tell him. "Someone gave me some photos yesterday," she said. "From my birthday celebration at school. I've been teaching for twenty years, so it was a sort of anniversary celebration as well. It all went really well, and I had a lovely time."

He dutifully sat down to look at the photos. It would have been impossible to refuse. A cup of tea, a courteous glance through the pages of the album – this was more important than the cupboards. He felt obliged to smile politely as he looked at the assortment of cheap multicoloured sweaters the teachers were wearing and read the birthday poems they'd written in her honour, one of which was particularly mawkish.

"Did a Russian teacher write that one, by any chance?" joked Pavel and immediately regretted it, because Anna Mikhailovna took his question seriously.

"No, the Technologist... He's very talented, you know. You should see the spoons he makes! I've got a whole set of them."

The piano stood silently on the other side of the wall. At least he didn't have to move that as well.

Suddenly one of the photos caught Pavel's eye. "Is that your assembly hall?" he asked.

In the photo Anna Mikhailovna, visibly moved, was standing in front of a red curtain that looked heavy enough to smother you in an earthquake. The velvet had gone dark in places and some of the marks on it looked like handprints, which made it look vaguely like the backdrop to a murder scene. There were some cheerful cardboard letters pinned above the curtain; Pavel couldn't read them, but he knew he'd seen them before. He'd been in this very hall, and quite recently.

"Which school do you work at?"

"Number Ninety."

"But that's here, on the corner of Sofya Perovska Street, isn't it?"

He hadn't anticipated this. When he, Maxim and Elya had pulled up in the school courtyard, which was completely flooded with orange light (a universal measure that appeared to have been introduced after the Beslan school massacre), Pavel recognized it as Natasha's neighbourhood. He had made a mental note to ask her whether she'd studied there. It hadn't even occurred to him that Anna Mikhailovna might have worked there.

From the very beginning he hadn't really understood the point of the trip. Maxim explained that it was company policy to organize "informal meetings" every week or two, where their clients were invited to have a drink and socialize. They hired a large hall for the occasion (whichever happened to be free on the evening in question), such as the local House of Culture, a school or a technical college.

Who the hell cares, thought Pavel, in gloomy disbelief. He had been asked to wear a white shirt, seeing as he didn't own a light-coloured suit. Maxim did, of course, and even Elya was wearing a white blouse.

It turned out that lots of people cared. About forty turned up: respectable men, important women. They all took their seats ceremoniously in the assembly hall. It took Pavel a while to notice that every single one of them was wearing light-coloured clothing.

When Maxim took his place at the lectern and began to speak, Pavel lost all sense of reality. Gone were the smirks, the cynicism. Maxim was deadly serious as he stood there and delivered his sermon, entrancing everyone in the room. You couldn't help but be fascinated by his inflection and delivery.

"We are the power! We are all successful people, the most important people in this city! Our achievements in life are not down to luck or circumstances. There is no such thing as luck! No, it's all because of our karma. We attract success! And furthermore, it is no coincidence that we are gathered here today..."

Maxim kept on speaking. One moment he was captivating the audience with his fluctuating intonation, the next he was stern and serious, staring intently around the room as though he were trying to imprint the words on their brains. Pavel tried in vain to catch his attention. He couldn't work out what was going on. Was it some kind of show? A psychology workshop? Was this how Maxim spent his spare time, when he wasn't working in the aviation industry – by trying to make a name for himself as a psychic healer? In fact, it soon became clear to Pavel that Maxim's performance was very closely related to the aviation industry indeed.

"We are protected by our karma! We will not fall, because we cannot fail! This applies to everything in life, but most of all to air travel. Aviation accidents do not occur by chance. Problems only arise in aircraft carrying passengers whose karma is weak and incompatible with life. Not like ours! Our aircraft will never be involved in any incident, no matter how minor. ARTavia aircraft are more than one hundred per cent reliable, and this is not only because we have the best aircraft, the best crew and the most comprehensive system of preflight checks – it is because we are the ones who make it so! Our success in life protects us from failure, and if we cannot fail – we will not fall!"

"It's like the mad leading the mad," Pavel whispered to himself, consciously distancing himself from the delusion. He was struck by the incongruity of the contrast between the gaudy school assembly hall and the deadly seriousness of the audience, between Maxim's inspired expression and his habitual worldly cynicism.

"We will not fall! We will not fall!"

Momentarily surrendering, Pavel was almost knocked off his chair by muffled waves of noise: the entire audience was solemnly repeating this invocation, heads bowed and eyes closed. They were all swaying and chanting, swaying and chanting, as though they were boarding up a casket.

Although Pavel was in the back row and therefore looking at them from behind, he recognized several individuals from the local TV channel, which was garish and loud and featured a lot of tabloid talk shows. On the whole, the audience was extremely diverse. There was an obese woman wearing enormous rings, who had an extravagant bouffant hairstyle. An attractive young woman, with her laptop resting against the chair in front. A gay couple. The man sitting directly in front of Pavel had a thick crimson neck, which was evidently constricted by the collar of his shirt. No doubt he was the veteran of a number of epic encounters, as a result of which he had managed to move up in the world. The usual story, from rags to riches.

The collective prayer came to an end. People struck up animated conversations with their neighbours, but there was also a palpable air of relief.

"Ladies and gentlemen, and now – a little coffee break!" Maxim changed his tone from ardent to urbane as easily as he changed jackets. "The lovely Elya will look after you."

The lovely Elya was looking a bit flustered. She might have been having a little trouble with the electric kettle in the school caretaker's room.

Meanwhile the lovely Maxim was drinking mineral water, his Adam's apple bobbing up and down. He caught Pavel's eye and winked. His expression gave nothing away.

CHAPTER 6

His taxi was already waiting at the stand, its exhaust fumes spilling furtively onto the tarmac, refusing to dissipate – a measure of how cold it was.

The new Volga bristled with chrome. It was a kind of greenish yellow colour, which reminded Pavel unpleasantly of a sinus infection. People had stopped using these state taxis some time ago because they were so expensive, and now they slumbered in rows at one end of the station, like crocodiles in the sun. But when the necessity arose, these were the transport of choice for ARTavia representatives. It would hardly be appropriate to turn up for a meeting with a client in some rusty old Zhiguli they'd flagged down in the street.

"Do you know the village of Red Springs?" asked Pavel, pulling the door open and getting in. The driver nodded.

The inside of the Volga smelled like the inside of a Volga always smells. For some reason Pavel was reminded of a story that had been all over the news several years earlier: when war broke out in Iraq one of the victims in Russia was the car manufacturer GAZ, because they had been about to supply a consignment of 300 Volga taxis, the epitome of socialist luxury, to Saddam's regime. For some reason, no one even dared to hope that the American occupiers might buy them instead. The press presented the situation as a tragedy – showing rows of greenish yellow cars standing idle, their chrome gleaming, their heavyweight elegance undiminished – and the authorities were deeply disgruntled. As though keeping these 300 Volgas in Russia would be a national disaster.

"Do you live in Red Springs, then?" asked the driver, as they drove down the main street.

"Are you kidding? Do I look like an oligarch?"

They both laughed. Their destination was a village of so-called cottages, which were actually more like mansions.

"Pavel, I've got a very important job for you today," Maxim had said that morning. He took out some paperwork. "You must convert to our faith a girl from a very noble family."

"Yes, Holy Father," Pavel bowed his head. They both roared with laughter.

"No, seriously. Do you know Mr Lvov?"

Of course he did. Everybody knew him. Evgeny Borisovich Lvov was a well known figure in the city who occasionally appeared in the national press, particularly when there was a heated political debate going on and dubious flyers were being distributed. He had friends in high places, having previously represented the region at the Federation Council. He was also a businessman, the co-owner of a car factory. A Very Important Person.

"Well, he has a daughter. She flies occasionally, sometimes to Moscow, and guess who her father has decided she'll be flying with from now on?" Maxim gave a slight smile. He allowed himself a modicum of irony. "Daddy Dearest wants to make sure she's completely safe, and that's why he came to us. So you're going to go to their house and get his daughter to fill in the forms for her gold membership card. It's already been paid for. He paid in advance, the day he came to see us. Everyone knows that a complete guarantee of safety doesn't come for free!"

Pavel took the forms and looked through them. Olga Evgenievna Lvova. Twenty years old. Studying at a local university... That was odd.

"Why isn't she studying in Moscow? Or somewhere like Pittsburgh?"

"No idea," Maxim replied with a shrug. "She obviously doesn't need to. Her father doesn't need her to, either. Or maybe he just wants to keep an eye on her."

Odd. Or was it? Maybe this unpretentious approach was actually the normal way of doing things? As opposed to Natasha's international ambitions and readiness to throw everything else overboard like ballast.

Pavel sighed. The taxi driver glanced at him. They had been stuck for what felt like forever at a completely ridiculous set of traffic lights.

Something wasn't right between them. In fact, nothing was right. His conversations with Natasha were going from bad to worse. Yesterday she hadn't even called, and the day before she had been agitated and keen to end the conversation. He even (briefly) entertained the crazy idea that over there, alone, she might have met someone else. One of her new classmates. An American. No, that was stupid. But everything had been fine when they were together, whereas over there he was largely out of sight and therefore a vacancy had arisen.

Pavel knew that it was nonsense (he grinned bitterly at himself in the foggy mirror, which also had a greenish tinge), but that didn't make it any easier. Everything was collapsing, all the fragile barricades he had naively tried to erect against Fate.

"You'd better put your seatbelt on," said the driver.

They were driving out of the city, past the traffic police checkpoint where this formality was still required, so Pavel obediently strapped himself in.

He was becoming increasingly aware that this step he'd taken in desperation – throwing himself into business in order to keep himself occupied, to show that he too had resolve and determination, to become worthy of her – was not yielding the desired results. The clearer the realization, the more he wanted to smash his forehead into the windscreen. Pavel's new life – working in the aviation industry (with a decent salary, incidentally) and spending every evening on Skype – reminded him of the film *Groundhog Day*. Every day, exactly the same.

Even Maxim had started to annoy Pavel, with his "king of the world" swagger and the way everything was such a joke to him. It was all a bit... American, which only added insult to Pavel's injury. It was almost as though he were overcompensating for some kind of hidden disability, like artificial limbs or blindness. Some blind people are so accustomed to life without sight that their impairment is not immediately obvious, though you can still sense that there's something different about them. Pavel presumed that Maxim had never suffered heartache, that maybe he'd never even been in love. Unless someone has also been burned by this fire, it is impossible to relate to them as an equal.

"Here we are," announced the driver.

On the other side of the metal gate stood a Mercedes with its engine running, indicators flaring up like adrenal glands. So there was a Mercedes, for starters. There were bound to be a couple of Sony PlayStations inside.

"Thanks. How much do I owe you?"

Surprisingly, the Lvov residence – a squat building painted yellowish grey, with curtains at the window – looked more like a real cottage than a mansion from the outside. Pavel was obviously expected. The gate opened as soon as he gave his name, and an unattractive, unremarkable individual wearing a black suit looked through his paperwork in a strange hall with a wide staircase. Lacquered wooden banisters, a mezzanine floor... It looked like the inside of a cupboard, apparently deliberately so. There was not a single personal item in sight, not even so much as a discarded newspaper.

Olga Lvova, a pretty brown-haired girl with rounded cheeks and a fringe, was watching a film in the living room. Pavel's escort addressed her by name and patronymic as they entered, and Pavel himself coughed in greeting. Just at that moment violin music soared from the network of speakers as the bandages were ceremoniously unwrapped from the woman's head on screen, revealing cropped black hair. "Congratulations," said the screen doctor, and the woman was handed a mirror. It was angled towards the camera so as to achieve the most effective shot, capturing bruised and swollen eyes, impossibly arched eyebrows and skin almost jaundiced from an excess of make-up. Pavel recognized it as a scene from *The Starling and the Lyre*, which he himself had seen quite recently. The TV channels were celebrating the 105th anniversary of the actress Lyubov Orlova's birthday and they all seemed strangely fond of this particular film. It wasn't even one of her best.

"Are you from Aeroflot?" Olga asked with a smile. "Hello, come in... Papa told me you were coming."

"Thanks, only I'm not from Aeroflot," replied Pavel, suddenly flustered. He even bowed slightly as he spoke. "I'm from ARTavia. My name's Pavel, and I'm here to deliver your gold membership card. We offer a great package. For example, any time you want to..."

"Too much information," said Olga, waving her hand dismissively. "Personally, I don't really care which airline I fly with. The safety issue doesn't bother me in the slightest. Would you like some tea?"

"Yes, please. But I'm afraid I'm obliged to tell you about the services that our company offers. Don't worry, I'll keep it brief!" said Pavel.

Meanwhile the woman on screen was changing her wig and her outfit, adopting various disguises, in a series of rotating images reminiscent of an old-fashioned kaleidoscope. There was something indisputably poignant about the actress disappearing like this. She kept glancing coyly to the side like a bird and screwing up her eyes, both gestures that would have been more appropriate in the age of silent cinema. Whenever she left the scene the set looked cheap and insubstantial, as though it were made of cardboard. Of course the film wasn't really about Soviet spies working undercover in wartime Germany; it was about Orlova's expression, the turn of her head, the way she held out her gloved hand to be kissed and the stylish way she slammed the door of the Mercedes as the raindrops rolled off it.

"Do you like Lyubov Orlova?" asked Olga, catching Pavel's eye. There was an almost mocking tone to her voice.

"I guess so... Not in *The Starling and the Lyre*, though."

"I've always liked her, ever since I was a little girl," said Olga, and she suddenly burst into a very accurate rendition of one of Orlova's signature songs. Pavel almost fell off his chair in surprise, and they both burst out laughing.

"But *The Starling and the Lyre* is a disgrace," continued Olga, suddenly scathing. "Playing a young woman at the age of seventy! The way she hides her face in a bunch of flowers, even when she's speaking."

"I can't help feeling sorry for her," Pavel said earnestly, taking himself by surprise. "I mean sure, she's a film star, but what kind of roles was she famous for? All that singing and dancing, mostly light-hearted stuff... At least she finally tried to take on a serious role. Same with her husband, Aleksandrov, who directed it. It wasn't their fault that by the 1960s and 1970s they were already out of touch with the new reality."

Pavel was quite interested in Soviet cinema, but he was worried that he'd picked the wrong time and place to enter into a debate about it. Then he noticed Olga looking at him attentively, as though she were seeing him for the first time.

"How can you say it wasn't their fault? It was pretty much a calculated career move on Aleksandrov's part. He made films whenever he felt like it, raked in a load of money, then spent a decade resting on his laurels. He built himself a mansion, and that was it – cinema had served its purpose. Then when he was already past it, he chose to embarrass himself by making this huge flop. I bet his savings had run out. To be fair, I don't think it was like that for Orlova."

Olga spoke with surprisingly genuine passion, but Pavel couldn't help feeling a sense of irony as he heard the words "money" and "mansion" used so disparagingly. After all, where were they right now?

"But I respect them both for the fact that they decided to do it at all," he retorted. "Okay, so it's a pile of crap – sorry, but I still respect them for it. They must have had enough money to be able to just sit there doing nothing for the rest of their lives, but instead they decided to make one final film, to die doing something they loved. They risked everything – their names, their reputation, their health, whatever – and they lost it all. But at least they took the risk. Look at the number of face-lifts Orlova had, everything she went through to preserve her beauty, only to ruin it all with harsh lighting and too much make-up. Then she fell ill, and then she died."

"Her heart and soul translated directly into this film!" Olga joked, and Pavel was relieved, because even while he was speaking he had been desperately thinking of a way to reduce the intensity of their conversation.

"You're a knight in shining armour," Olga smiled. "Defending old ladies' honour!"

"One old lady's, if you like. I just respect people who have an aim in life. A dream, a goal, whatever it might be.

Something that motivates them, for which they're prepared to take risks, to sacrifice everything... Or whatever."

He was losing interest now. They were done with the gold card. He wasn't going to get that cup of tea after all.

Olga saw him to the door. "Thank you! To be honest, I never expected to meet such an interesting..." She paused.

"Courier?" suggested Pavel, with a laugh. Olga protested, then also laughed. And that's how they parted, on the best of terms.

A nice chat is all well and good, but even "interesting couriers" need to make their way home from elite suburbs somehow. Pavel hadn't had the forethought – or rather, the inclination – to call a taxi from the Lvov mansion (he would have had to sit there even longer while he waited for it to turn up). So now, disconcerted, he found himself walking along a pristine concrete strip flanked by fences on both sides and followed it all the way to the highway. It was pristine, and apparently lifeless: he couldn't hear a thing, although he could sense security cameras following him as he passed. He had been here (or somewhere very like it) when he was younger, when the fashion for country cottages was in its infancy. Back then it had been a desolate expanse of grey concrete; even the children's playgrounds in the courtyards looked like building sites. It had been deserted then too but far from quiet, as the courtyards resounded with the eerie howling of stray dogs.

On that same day, 19 February 2007, a Boeing-757 flying from Krasnoyarsk to Moscow was forced to make an emergency landing. According to the Russian International News Agency, the airline KrasAir issued a press release confirming that there were 136 passengers on board. The air conditioning system's alarm sounded shortly after take-off,

and the pilot decided to return to Krasnoyarsk's Emelyanovo
airport. There were no casualties.

Pavel was feeling a growing sense of irritation – with the taxi
he hadn't called, with the car he hadn't managed to flag down,
with the dull, feverish light in the small Soviet-era bus that
had stopped to pick him up in the industrial part of the city. He
was the only passenger at the stop, and by this point he was
feeling thoroughly burdened by his suit and tie. The bus drove
beneath some futuristic-looking pipes wrapped in padded
silver insulation, braked obediently where the road crossed the
narrow-gauge rail tracks and filled up with commuters. The
journey felt all the more absurd because just one hour ago he'd
been arguing about a celebrated Soviet actress who had lived
in a world of fur coats and cinematic mansions, whilst actually
sitting in a mansion that was admittedly more modest but at
the same time more real. The lights in the bus were fading
and flaring according to its speed. This was making Pavel feel
sick, so he welcomed the distraction of a phone call from the
outside world. It was Igor.

"Can you come over?" Igor sounded desperate.
Lowering his voice, he added, "Danil's in a bad way."

"Is he sick?"

"Not exactly... Just come over, okay?"

"I'm on my way," answered Pavel. He tried to work out
where he was. They'd already reached the city, and he leapt
purposefully from one minibus taxi to another, like King
Kong in New York.

Danil was asleep in a dark room. At least, he was lying
down. Igor's face was so serious and sorrowful that Pavel
snapped, "What the hell's going on?"

"See for yourself," said Igor, leading him over to the
computer. The screen showed a page of *Soviet Chuvashia*,

the local newspaper in Cheboksary. Pavel didn't understand what all the fuss was about until he read the text.

The main perpetrators of the brutal murder that shocked Cheboksary had apparently served their time and been released from prison. Nearly ten years had gone by, and everyone had forgotten about it. Except, of course, the parents of the teenage victim. Quite elderly now, they had gone along to the editorial office where they were grateful for everything they were offered – a chair, a cup of tea – and spent a long time talking, repeating themselves, maintaining that the sentences were unjustifiably short in the first place, that several of the perpetrators had had their sentences reduced and that some were not punished at all. The journalists couldn't help the elderly couple. All they could do was to print a short interview in the hope that it might at least afford them some comfort. They printed names, too. Including Danil's, who was described as "one of the monsters" who got off "scot-free".

The article wasn't particularly recent, and it wasn't clear how it came to be on Danil's computer. Igor's theory was that a well-wisher must have sent it by email. He had found Danil already drunk and thoroughly depressed.

"What should we do?"

"I don't know. Let him sleep for now. Maybe we should get some normal food in? He's been eating all kinds of junk lately."

"Listen to us, like a couple of old women," joked Pavel, and they walked to the nearest shop where they bought grilled chicken, various salads and wine. In the gathering twilight the street lamps shone so brightly that it hurt to look at them, and exhausted workers crowded at the tills. Pavel was tired too. It had been a long day. He could feel his shirt growing damp where it was in close contact with his armpits.

They sat in the kitchen, half-heartedly sipping wine.

"I've never seen him like this before," said Igor, his voice faltering. Even now he couldn't help exaggerating for effect, playing the troubled writer. "There were actually tears in his eyes! I couldn't believe it. He was shaking all over and kept saying, 'How much more do I have to put up with? How much more?'"

"You know, I can sort of understand the parents," objected Pavel, trying to keep his voice down. He couldn't get the newspaper photograph out of his head: the frail and pitiable smiles of two broken people.

"Absolutely! Fair point, but Danil was just a child, and he didn't... Well, you know the story. He's spent his entire life as an outcast. People are still judging him, even now, and he's put up with it so far but..."

"But one of these days he's going to explode?"

"Exactly. And it could happen any time."

It was already dark when Danil got up, gloomy and disorientated, as though he'd lost all idea of time. Where was he? What day was it? He had something to eat and drink but he wouldn't speak, despite his friends' efforts to engage him in conversation.

They had to find something to distract him and cheer him up, urgently.

"Do you fancy going to Moscow with me?" suggested Pavel.

"You're going to Moscow?"

It was Maxim's idea. ARTavia's head office was organizing another two-day course for its regional managers – primarily for the new recruits – to refine their techniques of suggestion, persuasion and influence. In other words, "client relationship management".

"Why don't you go?" Maxim had suggested the other

day, after receiving the circular. "You won't learn much, of course, but you'll get a free city break out of it." The idea was to fly on a company plane and to stay in the company hotel ("Don't get too excited, it's more like a student hostel.") so it wouldn't cost him anything. The main thing was that there were two tickets for each region. "You can take your girlfriend, have some fun in the capital. No one else can go anyway, so you might as well." Pavel frowned. He couldn't work out whether Maxim had forgotten that his girlfriend was in America (he'd told him once), or whether he was deliberately trying to wind him up.

"So you could come with me," Pavel concluded. "Otherwise the airline ticket and hotel booking will only go to waste."

Danil glumly declined. "I don't feel like it, to be honest. Thanks for the offer... but why would I want to go to Moscow?" They couldn't reach him. His jaw was set in a determined manner, and the defences were up.

"Well, it's up to you. Call me if you change your mind."

CHAPTER 7

Igor went with him in the end. They decided to share a taxi to the airport, even though they didn't live anywhere near one another, because the airport was a long way outside the city – almost half an hour beyond the traffic police checkpoints, even taking into account the speed you could drive at that time in the morning, when the highways were deserted. Telegraph poles and street lamps flashed past, the latter flooding their surroundings with copper-coloured light, and the road stretched ahead like copper wire across the melancholy black fields. Every now and then a tiny light would appear in the distance, glowing like the moon.

Farms, possibly an electricity substation. Pavel watched them go by, staring at them with a strange and slightly uneasy intensity, the kind that results from having had only three hours' sleep.

After finding out that it would be cheaper to travel to the airport together, one of them picking up the other en route, Igor had enthusiastically suggested that they stay up all night: once they were packed and ready to go, they would meet at Danil's place for a drinking session and then go straight to the airport the following morning, without sobering up/sleeping/regaining consciousness.

"You're an idiot," declared Pavel.

"Why?"

"This is a business trip for me, not a trip to Disneyland!"

He was reminded of the Disneyhell conversation with Maxim.

So there was no all-night drinking session, but Igor's eyes still shone in the darkness with a gleam of anticipation (he had been picked up second and was therefore relegated to the back seat). This was a huge adventure for him. Flying to Moscow on the spur of the moment, for a couple of days, without even taking a bag! He was almost giddy with excitement. Pavel knew that he was being a bit hard on Igor and tried to control himself, suppressing his irony and peering out of the window at the dance of the dazed street lamps instead. Igor had his own reasons for going to Moscow. The night they'd first discussed the trip to Moscow, when Pavel had been so uncomfortable in his suit, Igor had admitted that he'd been plucking up the courage to take the plunge and pitch his fantasy drivel to a couple of literary magazines in Moscow. Affecting a casual nonchalance, he'd mentioned *Novy Mir* and *Znamya*. If he didn't do it now, he might not get another chance. Once he'd made up his mind he even seemed to sit a little taller. Having a purpose in life definitely makes a person more attractive.

They arrived in Moscow. The name of the city was emblazoned throughout the arrivals hall in a strange font, some letters narrow and others wide, a legacy of the 1960s, that auspicious pre-computer era, when pictures of the heroic cosmonauts were hand-drawn in the newspapers with pen and ink.

"So, shall we have a beer then?" said Igor.

An overweight female border guard wearing too much make-up was pretending to study their passports.

"It's six o'clock in the morning!" exclaimed Pavel, exasperated.

Maybe he should have come alone after all.

They ended up in the airport café, which was full of hungover, dishevelled passengers in transit. A time and place like no other. Circumstances in which even a respectable person would permit himself a shot of vodka: (a) early in the morning, (b) alone and (c) exposed to the world in a brightly lit glass-walled café, surrounded by dark fields and open spaces. Surrounded by the enormous black openness of space. The gates of Heaven wide open. Behind the counter, which was smeared with dried-out salmon roe, sat an exhausted café attendant, utterly defenceless against the backdrop of this vast black sea. Still it felt good to be there, surrounded by people, before stepping into the sky.

The Tupolev aircraft swayed lazily at their moorings, barely fastened to the ground.

Concentrating hard, everyone listened to the flight announcements. Five of the next six flights were for Moscow. Different airlines. Various Moscow-bound travellers trooped out of the airport cafés at ten minute intervals, all eyeing one another. Who were the lucky ones? They would be just the same on the shuttle buses, casting a critical eye over other Moscow-bound planes that they passed on the way to their own.

They ordered two pints of Guinness. Pavel cheered up a bit as he sipped the bitter liquid and chewed on a lukewarm pie. Things between him and Natasha were just as they should be. Air travel, different continents, Skype – that was life in the twenty-first century! They were successful, modern people. They were still together, whether they were in Moscow or the States, or... Yes, they would fly together and fly apart. Snatching an evening together whenever they had the chance, a nice restaurant, music, words tumbling out as they caught up on all their news... Would they fly apart again afterwards? So what if they did. Theirs was the happiness of people who were going places. Life was brighter this way than stuck in a joyless, monotonous, inadequate, mutually destructive marriage.

"There's something strange about this pie," Igor observed thoughtfully.

Igor had written his first proper story in the eighth grade, when he was about fourteen. He'd written things before then, of course, and he'd been soiling paper since early childhood. (He would never forget the immaculate reams of typing paper – pearly white, pink and pale blue – that his mother would bring home from the local government offices where she worked, because paper was one of many deficit commodities at the time. He had been fascinated by them.) Clumsy sketches and crude comic strips. A wordy imitation of a popular detective series for children. His esteemed family gushed with praise, and at some point they must simply have gone too far.

But in the eighth grade something serious spilled from his pen, which may have had something to do with the fact that Igor was seriously upset at the time. He was sick of being the butt of everyone's jokes and spent his time devising ways to solve the problem, such as keeping his mouth shut more often (literally), refraining from making smart remarks (easier said than done) and looking stern.

Igor had been the class clown since he'd started high school, but he'd only just started to realize that nobody took him seriously, that he didn't have any real friends, that life was passing him by. These days we're overexposed to life on our TV screens but back then, amongst Igor's teenage classmates, it had just begun to flourish for real: friendships, relationships, romance. Meanwhile Igor went about like a tragic hero from Russian literature, wearing a soldier's greatcoat, watching from the sidelines, still a source of amusement to others but discovering within himself a sensitive, romantic soul. Igor's favourite song at the time (a prime example of sentimental 1990s pop music) was popular with at least half the class, but he would never have admitted that he liked it too; instead he made a show of mocking its inane lyrics at the school disco. At home he had secret hoards of cassette tapes that he'd either bought or clumsily recorded from the radio, but he would have been mortified if anyone had ever found one of his tapes and heard what was on it.

It was a shame that story hadn't survived. The corners of Igor's mouth turned up in a half-smile as he watched himself disappearing in the gigantic airport window. It was getting light. The reason the story hadn't survived was because every couple of years or so Igor was seized by a furious desire to erase his past work, his imperfect efforts, and to start once more at the beginning of the path to genius. Layers of cultural history, entire strata of writing paper fell into the rubbish tip. Even his parents lamented aloud, almost genuinely.

They were late boarding, and the shuttle bus barely made a noise as it carried them between the slumbering elephantine Tupolevs. Mist hovered above the concrete. Their plane was waiting for them. The turbines were rotating slowly, making a whistling noise. They stood there taking small gulps of icy air, breathing out steam, quietly talking, waiting. Somebody once said that the Tu-154 was the last aircraft that actually looked like a jet. It was undeniably attractive, with its sleek design and romantic aesthetics. Pavel couldn't help but appreciate this as he stood there, freezing, at the foot of the gangway.

The VIP passengers didn't exactly look the part as they stood there stamping their feet by the antediluvian gangway, which was like something out of a Soviet cartoon. Someone flicked away a cigarette butt and the wind blew it under the giant wheels. The whole point of an elite group is to distinguish its members from the general riff-raff, so when the whole plane is business class... The only exalted position was occupied by the flight attendant who stood by the door collecting the stubs of their boarding passes: a seasoned veteran of high winds, worldly wise. They boarded the aircraft in small groups. Before stepping into the enclosed world, Pavel slapped the aircraft's wet metal flank like a friend's shoulder, as if to say "don't let me down".

Nothing was going to go wrong, was it? Hang on... Had he actually started believing all that nonsense?

He and Igor were placed right at the back of the cabin, separated from the rest of humanity by five or six semi-toothless rows of seats. As soon as they began taxiing down the runway the flight attendant stood with her back to the curtains and gave a virtuoso performance as conductor of the aircraft, which essentially involved waving a fake oxygen mask about.

"Which stories are you taking to Moscow?" Pavel asked suddenly, with genuine interest, once they'd fastened their seatbelts and settled down for the flight. The plane was ascending sharply, making the little curtains hang at an angle, and turning so that the distorted forests below rose up on one side. It made you want to focus on the back of the chair in front of you and not think about anything.

The first time the local newspaper printed one of Igor's stories was during a dry, crimson autumn, just after he'd entered the tenth grade. It led to instant and enduring fame, since the newspaper page in question was hung on a stand in the school library. Igor secretly recorded the comments of his female classmates and put up with the teasing of his male classmates, who urged him to spend his fee on a round of strong beer to toast his success. (He kept quiet about the fact that the fee didn't cover the cost of the beer, so he'd ended up out of pocket.) This experience led, via a PE lesson, to Igor's career in journalism.

The PE teacher suggested that, since Igor already had his name in print, he could write a short article celebrating the school team's recent successes in local tournaments (the underlying message being that this was better than wasting print space on stupid stories). This was rewarded by leniency in PE, in which Igor was never likely to get above a C grade and was regularly taunted for being overweight. Replacing one ritual humiliation with another, Igor went back to the editorial office time and time again.

Igor hated the PE teacher with all his heart. Meanwhile the PE teacher himself grew increasingly enthusiastic about their arrangement. He got into the habit of sitting down during basketball practice next to Igor (who was alone on the sidelines, having been excused from outdoor games) and discussing the controversial journalist Sergei Dorenko and his recent TV broadcasts. Or simply repeating fragments in his own words, minus the swearing. One day he sat down, reeking of sweat and garlic, and said that he'd dozed off while watching Dorenko (I bet he was drunk, thought Igor) and had woken up to find the screen blank. Suppressing his revulsion, Igor explained what everyone else already knew: that the local governor had ordered the broadcast to be cut in mid-transmission. The PE teacher was delighted that the mystery had been solved. Igor smiled scornfully, then walked with the other sweaty pupils to the changing room.

These were the complicated paths that led Igor to journalism and literature. They were all the more circuitous because of a certain scandal and Igor's subsequent failure to get into the Philology department. He had spent six months dealing with the Head of Department, a malodorous professor, with whom he hadn't exactly hit it off. (The professor had barely glanced at the newspaper clippings that Igor had proudly brought in to show him.) Then he was caught cheating and kicked out of the entrance exam. He left the building with a stiff upper lip, while the malodorous professor stared out of the window. In desperation his parents submitted his documents to the Social Studies and Humanities department, which still had places available... but that's another story.

Igor rested his forehead against the endless, icy tundra in the sky. At this height the sky outside the window was the colour of a watermelon.

When they reached the clear skies above Moscow they spent a long time circling over the airport, which they only knew because of the blinding morning sun. Youthful and predatory, it peeped into the cabin at one side then the other, slowly sliding down the frozen faces. Everyone was tense and silent, and it occurred to Pavel that this was probably what it felt like just before a crash.

He expected Sheremetyevo to be a painful reminder of October, of his trip with Natasha, of Natasha herself. The pain wasn't exactly tormenting him, but... Pavel wasn't in fact suffering so much as aware that he was suffering and that this was how it should be. In the event it was fine, because they landed at a different terminal. The airport buses were like Martian spaceships, with all their clever features. It somehow offended him that modern technology should be subservient to such mundane, inert and outmoded aircraft.

Not having any luggage to speak of, Pavel and Igor were out of the airport in no time. They squeezed into a crowded minibus taxi, where their fellow passengers were stoically preparing themselves for the inevitable traffic jams on the way into the centre.

"I'm going to be in meetings all day," announced Pavel, in a brisk, business-like tone. "Why don't you go into town? Have a wander round."

He was about to bequeath to Igor his usual routes: Tverskaya with its towering sculpted facades, bristling with memorial plaques, the Moskva River embankment... Because Igor couldn't possibly have any of his own.

"I've got a few things to do myself, in case you'd forgotten!" Igor answered indignantly. He had spent the entire flight drumming his fingers on the bulging file he'd brought with him, which he now opened. Pavel couldn't help smiling at the naivety of the "city survival kit" that his friend took out: a calendar featuring a map of the metro and some newspaper clippings with the addresses and telephone numbers of various editorial departments. They had "USSR" printed on them. What the...

"Are those from old issues?"

"I don't know, I just found them at home."

"Didn't it occur to you that they might have moved, or shut down?"

"Damn!" Igor was genuinely flummoxed. "I didn't think to check online. I can check them here though, can't I? I assume they have internet cafés."

He really had taken the plunge, eyes closed, convinced that these prestigious literary magazines still existed, that they had survived the test of time. The world had started falling apart since Igor's parents, like all respectable members of the intelligentsia during the perestroika era, had subscribed to publications such as *Novy Mir* and *Znamya*. It wasn't clear what, if anything, remained. It was like the bit in a Hollywood disaster movie when a global catastrophe has occurred, plunging the world into darkness, and a plane or a boat has set out on a reconnaissance mission, but nothing is showing on the radar screen and the hero at the wheel has almost given up hope of finding anyone alive. Igor felt exactly the same as everyone else who had grown up in the provinces at the turn of the 21st century. He had printed out his best work and put it in a file, and now he was prepared to fight his way through to the other side, no matter what awaited him there.

Moscow descended on Pavel in the form of a headache. A consequence of his sleepless night, or the turbines and the altitude, or possibly the early-morning beer. He had bought some painkillers in the first dubious chemist he came across and taken them straight away, but he couldn't tell whether or not they had worked. The leaden feeling in his head was still there. Pavel approached the escalator in the metro station like a doomed man, walking beneath the military mosaics, feeling depressed at the prospect of spending a whole hour in rumbling tunnels. With a headache. He glanced about, trying to find something to distract his thoughts.

The guard on duty – an elderly woman with military bearing – stood in her little cubicle at the base of the escalator. She was talking into the receiver of a retro-style black Bakelite telephone from the 1940s, with a fabric-covered cord. It was strange that they hadn't replaced these old telephones. Strange, but cool. You could actually believe that the guard had a direct line to the 1940s. Whenever they show Putin and the others on TV, there always seem to be white disc-shaped telephones from the 1970s on the tables. (When journalists ask about them, which doesn't happen very often, they're always referred to as "contemporary electronic devices".) That's pretty cool, too.

One of the monuments at Novodevichy Cemetery consists of a granite communications marshal speaking into a granite telephone receiver, while the granite cord leads off into eternity, or so it seems.

Pavel sat down in between the platforms in the hope of soothing his head, just as a train burst out of one of the tunnels with a high-pitched wail, like a falling bomb. These old carriages were interesting, with their decorative excesses and elegant colouring and the modern handles on the doors at both ends. They could be thirty years old, or sixty. Why was that? By contrast an aircraft ages rapidly, turning a tired grey colour and developing dark patches around the turbines, like emerging schoolboy moustaches. But these carriages were timeless. Maybe it was because they had never known what it was like to make an effort; they had never known life on the surface, the freedom of open spaces.

The sky was a deep, dark blue by the time the "Seminar for Regional Managers" (Part One) ended. Pavel didn't feel like staying for the dinner so he called Igor and they went back to the hostel, which was conveniently located close to the domestic terminal of Sheremetyevo airport. The hostel (ARTavia made a big deal about it being a "company hotel", though the internal signage made it perfectly clear that theirs wasn't the company it belonged to) was not only cheap but nasty too. It smelt of damp neglect and burnt rags, and insects scuttled along the cracks between the tiles in the shower room. Igor made a crass joke about prisoners.

The kettle sang victoriously.

"Well, at least we're having fun!" declared Igor.

There was no chance of a quiet chat or an early night, because at the other end of their dormitory room (seven beds!) sat a group of men who clearly bore no resemblance to "regional managers". The men were drinking vodka, moderately but furtively; to all intents and purposes they were simply growing increasingly flushed, roaring with laughter and cutting slices from a garlic sausage.

Pavel sighed. He was tired. He contemplated pulling a sheet over himself to escape the glare of the greasy, dusty light bulb and giving in to sleep; the bus left for the seminar the following day at 8 a.m. Igor was also starting to get annoyed. This was apparent from the way he started questioning the men, albeit with an outwardly pleasant demeanour.

"So, are you all qualified pilots then?"

The men burst out laughing. It was hardly surprising that Igor had guessed their profession, as it was perfectly obvious from their conversation. No, what had amused them was his pompous tone of voice.

Igor remembered reading in a dictionary of associations that flying was connected with impotence. He smiled, as though this were his secret trump card. Aloud he asked, "Is it normal for pilots to drink like that?"

The men laughed again. Their cursory, contradictory responses covered the entire spectrum from "You call this drinking?" to "We're not flying tomorrow." They were already staring at Igor with interest, wondering who on earth he was. But Igor wouldn't let it lie, and the battle of words continued.

"Well, I read in the in-flight brochure this morning," Igor began despondently, "that ARTavia is the only carrier claiming to offer a one hundred per cent safety guarantee. Apparently this is due to high standards in terms of aircraft quality control and an extremely experienced crew, amongst other things. Apparently various safety checks and inspections are carried out before every flight, including medical examinations..."

At this point Pavel resigned himself to getting beaten up, along with Igor, but instead the room exploded with noise. The men were rolling about with laughter, making the metal bed frames creak.

"ARTavia! One hundred per cent! Oh, I've heard it all now... Numerous inspections... That's hilarious!"

"A one hundred per cent safety guarantee... You know that's total bullshit, right? They're just making it up, saying what the old farts want to hear. That's definitely something they're good at. One hundred per cent, indeed..."

Stretching his sizeable feet out in front of him, the tallest of the men spoke so seriously and with such passion that Pavel could only nod, mesmerized. He was simply relieved that there wasn't going to be a fight after all. The other men chimed in. Igor had touched a nerve. Triggered a reaction.

"Do you think that just because we're stuck in the cockpit we don't know what's going on? They tried to brainwash us with all that rubbish too, telling us what to say, how to convince people... It's practically hypnosis. Like some kind of sect. Well, you know what they're like!"

"No, I don't," retorted Igor. He wasn't ready to give up the fight.

"Well, their so-called high standards of aircraft quality control are basically nonexistent," remarked one of the other men, who had alarmingly close-set eyes. "Flying coffins, that's what they are!" They all grew serious. "They've leased a load of scrap metal from Central Asia, mainly Kazakhstan. Guys, this is the fifth airline I've worked for, if you include Soviet Aeroflot, and the condition of their planes is the worst I've ever seen! The wiring's such a mess, I'm almost afraid to touch the control panel."

"Yeah, you should see our logbook of postponed repairs. It's more hardcore than Goethe's fucking *Faust*! Or our Certificate of Airworthiness... It's like, you go into the cockpit before the flight and think, what the hell? Where is everything? It's all mixed up. The thrust reverse, the speedometer, the chassis hydraulics... Even the documents are a complete joke. Ha! We should sell them to the press, when it all goes tits up."

A peculiar, hollow laugh.

"Hang on," said Pavel, raising himself up on his bed. The conversation had begun to genuinely interest him. "We're all staying at the company hotel." (More raucous laughter.) "There's a seminar going on at the moment, and people have flown in specially for it. You can't possibly not realize that we might be connected to ARTavia in some way," said Pavel, struggling to follow his own convoluted syntax. "Aren't you worried about saying stuff like that to people you've only just met?"

He noticed that some of them looked a little wary – the ones who hadn't said much so far – but those who had been more outspoken remained undaunted. If anything, they became more aggressive.

"Why should I be worried? What have I got to lose? I don't care if I get fired. I've already been approached by Ural Line in Yekaterinburg. They want me to go and work for them, but this lot keep persuading me to stay. Even though they pay me peanuts! I've got a first class pilot's licence, not to mention the flight hours I've logged, but I can't even bring myself to tell you how little I earn – particularly over the holidays! It's nothing like what they promised. Meanwhile they're raking it in."

The pilots were so worked up by this point that it was pointless trying to calm them down. They carried on raging indignantly amongst themselves, and it looked as though they were going to be at it for some time.

"Huh," responded Igor, putting on a stupid voice. "And we've still got to fly back! Maybe we should get the train, eh, Pavel?"

Pavel ignored him because he was desperate to shut his eyes, to shut the world out completely... The only trouble was that the light bulb had found a way into his brain and kept tormenting it from inside.

CHAPTER 8

Watching planes fly... Many of us can remember this from childhood, particularly those of us who were taken to summer cottages near the airport, where planes would leave their tracks to unfurl in the sky above our heads. A deafening, otherworldly roar. The grown-ups would grumble but you would jump in delight, trying to leap away from the vegetable beds, waving your hands and wondering if the pilot had seen you. The plane was so low that you could see everything, as if it were a model, right down to the inscriptions and the wheels on the chassis.

It was a long time since Olga Lvova had known anything remotely resembling such delight. In any case, the roar of aircraft pressing on the windows was such a regular feature that it was barely noticeable. That was the stupidest thing about the elite village of Red Springs, that it had been built right next to the airport, and however hard they tried to soundproof the mansions... Well, you can get used to anything. But that morning it happened to be a plane that had woken Olga Lvova.

She lay there for a long time looking round her bedroom, which had a washed-out feel that morning. Everything outside was grey and a dry, papery snow was falling quietly. She could even hear the rustling sound it made, because the plane had passed and it was deathly silent once again.

In the summer, on a clear day, you could sometimes hear the high-pitched, almost mosquito-like whine of the highway.

Olga Lvova got up and went straight into her bathroom, where she frowned at the way her body bore the imprints of her tangled sheets, like a pattern stamped onto a biscuit. Then she went downstairs to breakfast.

The apartment where she'd been born was tiny, just a basic room in a communal apartment. Olga couldn't remember it herself, of course – her mother had told her about it. In those days Evgeny Borisovich Lvov had been a simple engineer at a machine building plant. Or maybe not that simple, as it turned out, given the way he'd managed to work his way up during the perestroika years by astutely opposing the corrupt, bureaucratic administration and expressing his views in print. His wife took care of little Olga, who was a sickly child, and had learned to accept their roller-coaster life: one day her husband was about to lose his job and they were faced with poverty and the threat of her child being kicked out of nursery school, the next he was suddenly a delegate at the 19th All-Union Party Conference and being elected into the new collective management of the factory.

Olga could remember their next apartment, which was large but strange. Back then, at the beginning of the 1990s, they couldn't even build elite accommodations properly. The builders must have been incompetent or lazy or both: crooked walls, cracks in the plaster, never-ending repairs, a cavernous lobby with metal doors... Half the building was visible from the windows like a sorrowful ruin, permanently floodlit. It was just one of many never-ending construction projects.

Her father barely featured in her childhood memories. She had the impression that he was hardly ever at home. She could remember him saying something about the governor inviting him to the *banya*, and she could remember him coming home late at night in a steamy car and giving her a hug, all drunkenly affectionate, giving her random presents because he didn't know what else to give her. He had brought a specific smell back from the banya, which tickled her throat.

She could remember one terrifying night, when she must have been about six or seven. Lights on throughout the house, toys scattered everywhere. There were people, scary people, wearing black balaclavas. Her father kept calling someone on the phone, shouting into the receiver. His hands were shaking, but he kept telling her that it was nothing to worry about, it was just a game.

Her mother stood there in silence, tears streaming down her face. The dog was going crazy in another room. They were trying to tidy up because one of the men had accidentally dropped a pot plant. A very ordinary-looking man in a suit, who wasn't wearing a mask, politely asked her mother, "Have you ever seen this before? We found this bullet in a glass in your sideboard."

Her mother automatically took what the man was holding out to her. Her father suddenly yelled at her in a terrible voice, "You fool! Now your fingerprints will be all over it! They brought it here with them and now you're holding it, you fool!"

Olga could remember this trivial scene well, because she had been offended on her mother's behalf. It was trivial because the bullet meant nothing after all, and it was never mentioned again. Why was it there in the first place? Her father was under a lot of pressure at the time to relinquish some shares, and eventually he did so. Olga found this out when she got older. She loved reading, and when she got older she suddenly started coming across similar incidents in books. Almost as though they were waiting to be discovered. Seen through the eyes of a child: 1937, an apartment being searched, the father led away, the child's last memory of him. These recurring scenes upset Olga dreadfully. It felt like a nightmare, as though someone had stolen her own memories.

It was the college holidays now, the heavy February rain was lashing against the window, and Olga had no idea whether or not she was enjoying this break from her studies. It wasn't like her schooldays. Not at all.

It wasn't that she was bored. On the contrary, she tried to fill every evening, not necessarily because she wanted to but to keep herself busy. So when something happened to scupper her plans...

"Olga Evgenievna?" said Mikhal Anatolych, in an expressionless voice that was perhaps not as polite as it could have been. He was one of her father's assistants – formerly his right-hand man, now fallen out of favour. In any case he was often around, either in the house or at the office, but only when his boss was absent. There was something unpleasantly reminiscent of Andropov about his face: the glasses, the nose.

"There's a car coming for you at 6.30 p.m. this evening, to take you to the Avant-Garde House of Culture."

She became aware of a familiar, mild ache in her forehead. This always happened when Olga's mood was abruptly spoiled. (Something to do with her blood pressure?) Just her luck: as soon as she made her own plans... Like today, there was a special screening at the Cinematika club. Olga wasn't even that bothered about going (and besides, she had no one to go with), but these unceremonious intrusions into her life on the flimsiest of pretexts had begun to irritate her more and more. This was the final straw.

"The Avant-Garde, did you say?"

Mikhal-Anatolych raised his eyebrows with a kind of puppet-like naivety. "Yes, the House of Culture. It's on... I can't remember the name of the street..."

"I know where it is," Olga interrupted him. "But what's the big occasion? A party, some sort of presentation?"

"Just a moment," he said, glancing into the bulging diary that he always carried around with him, apparently in order to make himself look important (whenever he needed to consult it outside, he would rip his glove off with his teeth, like an animal). "It's a meeting for ARTavia clients. You have to go."

"What do you mean, I 'have to go'?" Olga cried indignantly. "Why the hell should I? What's it got to do with me?"

"Evgeny Borisovich was most insistent," said Mikhal-Anatolych. He put only the slightest emphasis on the name of his boss, but it was still enough to make an impression. "He said that these meetings are very important, so you have to be there. Everyone goes..."

"Look," said Olga, speaking firmly despite her inner turmoil, "I'm not going anywhere. At least, not to some ridiculous meeting. I've already got plans for this evening!"

"Then perhaps you'd like to discuss the matter with Evgeny Borisovich," replied the assistant, demonstrating sphinx-like serenity.

"All right then, I will!" declared Olga, then she turned abruptly and flounced back to her room.

Changes in her father frightened her. During the course of her voracious reading (as mentioned above), she had once been struck by a passage in a book by Radzinsky. It was about Stalin's daughter, Svetlana Alliluyeva, and her relationship with the filmmaker Aleksei Kapler. Stalin was incensed to learn of his daughter's romance, mainly (according to the author) due to the unpleasant discovery that such romances were even possible. How could it be so, when Lenin's sister, Maria Ulyanova, was able to sacrifice her personal life in order to devote herself to Lenin?

Having recently come to see his only daughter as a potential asset to his business empire, there was a good chance that Evgeny Borisovich Lvov might react the same way.

He hadn't paid any attention to her until she was about fifteen − or rather, he hadn't taken her seriously. She could remember a number of stupid, childish things she had been upset about that her father had barely noticed. Once there was a prime-time program about him on TV, including a live interview, which everybody watched, including the ten-year-old Olga and her mother. When Evgeny Borisovich was asked which was more important to him, his work or his family, he immediately said work. Her mother had remained silent, but Olga could tell straight away how upset she was. Her grandmother on her father's side had called at that point, trying to make amends, repeating herself over and over again: take no notice, it's only television, the elections, that's just the way it is, he had no choice. That was just the way it was their whole life. But Olga never said anything. She didn't speak to her father for three days. What was the point? He was too busy at the time to be around much anyway.

Things began to change when they started having intense, heartfelt conversations about business, Russia, family and life in general. Unfortunately Olga didn't get around to selecting a specific career option before she reached her final year of high school, which, being an elite school, was inclined towards economics and business. So without any particular enthusiasm, but without any strenuous opposition either, she allowed her documents to be submitted to the Economics department on her behalf. Evgeny Borisovich took her to his office and initiated her into the world of business. He frequently referred to her as his helper and his successor.

Initially, when it was all within reason, Olga actually found it rather interesting. But then he started taking it too far, forcing her to try on this life as though it were borrowed clothes... Once, with an icy shudder, she decided to stage a protest, to tell him that she had other interests, that this wasn't for her. Instead of provoking a Stalinist fit of rage, her outburst merely met with mournful silence and an injured expression. And then before long it started all over again. She felt as though she were suffocating.

Evgeny Borisovich might have demanded to know what other interests she had. Olga would have simply stood there, mouth open, at a loss for words. How could she explain, for example, that her interest in 1930s world cinema was more than just a hobby? Or at least so she had convinced herself, in her desire to fill the emptiness.

As it went on this blind, incoherent feeling of opposition grew inside her, and more and more days were poisoned.

Like today. Olga was in a furious mood as she got ready to go to the Avant-Garde. She deliberately chose to wear a lurid green polo-neck sweater, because it seemed to express the way she felt.

"It says you're supposed to wear white," muttered Mikhal-Anatolych.

"What?"

"I mean, the fax... from ARTavia," he stammered. "It says that you're supposed to come in light-coloured clothing."

"Oh, just fuck off!" Olga slammed the door. Yes. That was the way to do it. Even if it was all she could do.

She could feel her stress levels rising. She wanted to take control, to make a decision of greater significance than whether or not to smoke another cigarette. In this frame of mind, she was delighted to bump into Pavel again at the Avant-Garde.

"So what's it like? Any good?" she whispered cheerfully.

"I don't know. I have to listen to it every week," Pavel answered conspiratorially.

After ten minutes or so Olga whispered, "Listen, I've got an idea. There's a special showing at Cinematika tonight. I was thinking of going... Do you want to come with me?"

This caught Pavel completely off guard. The way she'd addressed him in the familiar form, and the idea itself. In his current state of celibacy he never went anywhere, except to the temporary refuge of Danil's place, where the bathroom always smelt exactly like an old woman's bathroom in a Khrushchev-era apartment block: soapy rather than unpleasant, but somehow timeless.

"So, what do you reckon?"

"Well, I guess... okay then. What time does it start? Will we make it? Where is it, anyway?"

Maxim looked over at them, not for the first time.

"We'll be all right if we leave now."

"You mean, like, right now?"

Pavel didn't really know what he was doing. Before he even had time to think about it, they had pushed open the old carved door and found themselves in the echoing foyer.

"We'll have to go out through the back door," said Olga, looking around anxiously. "I had to bring a couple of bodyguards... And I don't want them tagging along!"

They emerged into a dark courtyard, where some old rubbish bags were leaking their putrid contents, then got on a light-blue trolleybus. Three stops later Olga was striding confidently through the back streets of the old centre, past surprisingly inviting red and yellow windows through which they glimpsed curtains, lamps, TV screens, and simple meals served straight from the frying pan.

Pavel's mobile phone rang. The display panel said "Maxim". Shit. Should he answer it? What would he say?

"I always switch mine off when I go AWOL," Olga remarked casually, over her shoulder. Pavel took the hint, but just switched it to silent mode.

They were a little late getting to the special screening at Cinematika, which turned out to be an ordinary pirate screening in a claustrophobic, out-of-the-way bar. The light behind the bar stayed on, making the whole place look like an aquarium. On screen two young men wearing ludicrous outfits – funnily enough, also in white – were behaving with increasing absurdity, from dropping eggs on the floor to murdering a family. It was Michael Haneke's *Funny Games*. Pavel hadn't seen it before, but he recognized the bit with the eggs from somewhere. On this side of the screen they were sitting at little tables, drinking shamelessly diluted beer. The room was almost full. Pavel thought about going to the bar but decided against it.

In the flickering light from the screen he glanced over at his companion, with her little snub nose and unusual, unfashionable fringe. She was pretty, nevertheless. Maybe even beautiful.

Eventually the interminable closing credits began to roll. This always reminded him of his childhood, in which third-rate action movies and the swapping of videocassettes had featured heavily. Back then he had been fascinated by the American style of arranging the words centrally in columns, and he used to wonder why Russian film-makers couldn't make theirs look as good. Now he just wondered what he'd ever thought was so great about it.

"Drink up, citizens, we're no longer serving and we're closing in twenty minutes!" came the shrill announcement from the girl behind the bar, enjoying her moment in the spotlight now that the Austrian actors had relinquished theirs.

"Shall we go somewhere else perhaps?" asked Olga. Misinterpreting Pavel's hesitation, she added, "Don't worry, I've got some cash on me."

"Don't be silly," said Pavel, coming to his senses. "I've got plenty."

"Sorry."

He glanced at his phone: shit, nine missed calls from Maxim! He had a feeling in the pit of his stomach that he'd made a huge mistake, that leaving the meeting had been a really stupid thing to do... but really, what was the big deal? It was too late to worry about it now anyway. As he switched his phone off completely Pavel felt short of breath, as though he'd just conquered Everest.

They remembered that there was an all-night coffee shop just two blocks away, which turned out to be open. It occupied the ground floor of an ancient brick building with arched windows (an impressive cast-iron staircase led up to the first floor, which housed the head offices of some kind of regional educational organization) and had been decorated inside to create a suitably historical atmosphere, with a dark wood trim, old-fashioned sideboards and a large clock over the entrance door. The place was virtually empty.

"So, what did you think of the film?" asked Olga, when their coffees and bowls of ice cream were placed in front of them.

The old-fashioned silk lampshade made her face (his too, of course) look as though it were made of wax, but even this was attractive. Like vintage postcards with old Russian lettering, where the yellowing of the card over time does not in any way detract from the beauty of the angels.

"I didn't like it, to be honest."

"Why not?" she asked, surprised.

"It's a pretty brutal film."

"I guess so," said Olga, frowning as though she were concentrating really hard on working out a complicated sum. "But you're not supposed to take it seriously. It's a deliberate device, a kind of in-joke…"

"I realize that," said Pavel, lifting the tiny cup to his mouth. "But still, I just can't watch stuff like that. I mean, obviously I can sit there and watch it, but it really bothers me. I don't know… Those psychos kill an eight-year-old boy, right? Then they leave, and his parents are trying to work out how to save themselves… the mother runs for help, right? While the father tries to fix the phone, by shaking the battery or something, I can't remember… And the whole time they're trying not to look into the corner where their son's body is, and it's so obvious that they're trying not to look. There's a good ten minutes of the father shaking the phone battery in close-up, and one minute he's crying, the next he's pulling himself together. It's all so contrived. I don't know... I just can't get my head around that sort of thing."

Olga had been listening attentively as she stirred her coffee, but now she interrupted impatiently.

"No, but it's a deliberate device, to provoke the viewer. You're not supposed to take it at face value. It's post-modernism, you know? Like when the family kill one of the intruders and the other one gets to rewind the film. Or the way we keep seeing the knife in the bottom of the boat and then suddenly they throw it overboard, and it's as if the gun was never fired. Directorial tricks like these, the way he mocks all the clichés – that's what I like about it."

"I know what you mean, but I just don't see it that way. For me when a film's that brutal, it's like a kind of barrier. I mean, killing a child in front of its parents, that kind of thing. I don't know... When it goes that far, I just don't think you can call it a device any more. But then, what do I know?" Pavel fell silent, then suddenly burst out laughing. "Ha! When they used to take us to the cinema in the fifth grade, they started off by showing us old propaganda reels. I've just remembered this one scene, when a boy ran out into the road at a red light and was hit by a Volga. It happened off screen, but he'd been carrying a bottle of *kefir* in a string bag and they showed it smashing on the tarmac, under the wheel. I couldn't bear the sight or the sound of it! My first thought was, what about his parents, and his grandparents? How are they going to tell them? I just sat there with my eyes closed, hoping no one would notice."

Olga laughed too with a palpable sense of relief, amused by this stark contrast to post-modernism.

Pavel suddenly pictured himself, happy and smiling, his face the warm yellow of a religious icon in the light from the lampshade, and was belatedly surprised that his new friend seemed to think he was some kind of film connoisseur. Where had she got that idea? From the conversation they'd had about Lyubov Orlova, with her skin pulled taut, excessive make-up and unfeasibly wide-open eyes? They had met again by chance, but Olga seemed to have been waiting for him to accompany her to this semi-underground showing and was now asking his opinion, almost humbly. He was no film connoisseur. Far from it! The girl from the mansion was mistaken, as she probably was in many other areas of life. Pavel was not a discerning cinema-goer; he would just watch the latest blockbuster as a matter of course, along with the rest of his generation. He remembered how, as teenagers, they would furtively gather in someone's apartment to pass around cans of beer and watch Russian gangster movies. *Fight Club*, too – the same primal joy of the mob mentality.

It was better that she didn't know the details.

Suddenly he was acutely conscious that she had invited him to see this particular film with her because it was a film that she liked, yet he was sitting there criticizing it, picking it apart with a condescending sneer on his face.

"No, no!" protested Olga, when he clumsily tried to explain. "You made some really interesting points."

They talked and smiled, talked and smiled again. They were the only customers left in the coffee shop now. The waiters were watching TV with the sound turned down and didn't seem to care. Paralyzed with dread and delight, Pavel tried to imagine what time it might be. (He was too scared to switch his phone back on.)

"So tell me about yourself, about your friends. What are they like?" asked Olga.

Pavel was completely flustered. What was he supposed to say? What would she think if he told her about Igor, for example?

"What about that young guy, the one who was speaking earlier?"

It took a while for him to realize that she was talking about Maxim. "Young guy", indeed! "Middle-aged gentleman", more like.

"Well, he's not really a friend... Actually, believe it or not, we're second cousins."

So Pavel told her about Maxim, about how he came from the middle of nowhere and had managed to get where he was today on his own merit, using his own hands, his own brains, his own teeth. Generally, when someone is cheerful, creative and optimistic, that counts for a lot in life. He had his eccentricities, of course, but who doesn't? For example, his obsession with politics. Only the day before Maxim had been driving him mad with his constant ranting about the closure of the controversial Ultra Kultura publishing house in St Petersburg, which had turned into a more general rant about the suppression of free speech, totalitarianism and other such fascinating subject matter.

"Papa calls people like that 'minus people'," declared Olga.

"What does he mean by that?"

Olga responded with a short speech that she'd obviously heard somewhere before, about how Russia's main problem was the fact that a significant proportion of the national elite (Olga repeated herself here, emphasizing the point) were always in opposition to the authorities, regardless of who was occupying the Kremlin: Putin, Yeltsin, whoever it might be. These individuals – the most influential businessmen, the most talented musicians, the most highly skilled IT experts, and so on – would oppose any measures introduced by the state on principle, even those that were vitally important. They would automatically kick up a fuss (again, Olga was at pains to emphasize the point) and do their level best to put a spanner in the works. They were always in opposition, hence the "minus". That was the country's main problem.

"In that case, surely they should be 'minus citizens'. Otherwise it sounds a bit Fascist!" Pavel grinned and Olga laughed, realizing that it was necessary to relieve the tension of the situation.

Pavel had begun to feel a little uncomfortable at the mention of Olga's father. Was it normal for her to stay out all night like this? He wondered whether she'd kept her phone on silent too.

"Why don't you tell me about your friends?" he suggested.

Olga hesitated. Who should she tell him about? Inna?

At school, Olga thought she got on well with everyone. She was friendly and kind; at least, that was how she saw herself. She liked looking at herself from the outside.

"You act like a character in a film, did you know that?" said the strange new girl, Inna, who was staring at her pointedly. They had got talking at one of the parties that were organized regularly for their class, with the encouragement of their well-to-do parents. If they were going to sleep around, they might as well do it within the group.

Olga didn't understand.

"You always look like you're acting, you know? Not in a contemporary film. These days it's all about real life and naturalistic acting, whereas you look like you're playing a role, like you're wearing a mask."

Inna was strangely uninhibited at the best of times, but that evening she was knocking back the semi-illicit cocktails and Olga wasn't entirely sure how to react, whether or not to be offended. But Inna was already chatting away about classic films.

A strange friendship developed out of this encounter. Olga started going round to visit her new friend, and together they would watch the films of Mary Pickford and Marlene Dietrich. It turned out that Inna had an enormous collection of DVDs (some of them quite rare), posters and memorabilia. It turned out that Inna had strange interests and obsessions, and this fascinated Olga. A new world, something new. They dressed up like Marlene Dietrich in *Blue Angel*, with top hats, cigarette holders and icy glances. They even shared a secret moment, which Olga herself could recall only vaguely, as though it had immediately been erased from her memory. Olga waited with bated breath for it all to blow up in a dreadful scandal, but in the end nothing happened: everything fizzled out and Inna disappeared. Her family moved to England, by all accounts.

But Olga's love of cinema remained, and she would never forget being told that she was like a character in a film.

CHAPTER 9

She was doing lots of new things, and at the same time doing other things completely differently. The logical conclusion (that she must have learnt it in America) suggested itself, but he drove it away, groaned and kept driving it away even now, exhausted as he was by the sadistically slow path traced by a single drop of sweat. The sex was wild. She was wild.

He shuddered as he thought about how much he'd missed Natasha's body and found the strength to distance himself for a second. Everything was the same: her small but beautiful breasts, nipples sticking out to the sides; her stomach rising and falling, as though she were panting for breath; and the finely shaven strip below with its playfully neat edges, like the sides of a matchbox. That he was about to strike...

They were entwined among the stiff sheets, twisted in places like a tourniquet, and she had wrapped her legs around him and was squeezing, squeezing, and kissing him like never before. The main difference was that she'd had her tongue pierced in America. Stroking metal with his tongue, Pavel was mildly surprised. Why this? Why now? Teen gimmicks weren't really her style. But then all extraneous thoughts, and all thoughts in general, receded.

Pavel shuddered.

Pavel came.

Pavel woke up.

It was ridiculous, but as a result of his nocturnal tossing and turning the silver cross he wore round his neck had somehow ended up in his mouth. A piece of metal. That was all.

The kitchen clock was ticking and the tap was dripping into the sink, but even so a tense, expectant silence hung in the air. Pavel began to feel uneasy. He lay there for a further ten minutes, gradually making sense of everything, trying to comprehend and differentiate between his strange, damp dream and the reality of the coffee shop the night before. He had overslept horrendously, of course. His parents had left some time ago. (In a daze, he got up and felt the side of the kettle, which was barely warm.) It was strange that work hadn't called. Or was it? Damn.

The back of his throat began to ache in anticipation of an almighty row. Because there was bound to be one. He didn't yet know exactly how he would end up paying for disappearing like that – for rejecting Maxim's calls and eventually, with a shiver, switching his phone off completely – and he couldn't explain why, but he somehow knew that it was all going to kick off. Big time. The silence of his phone today was even more ominous.

"Oh, what's the big deal?" Pavel felt unsettled in the empty apartment, so he decided to talk to himself as he made a cup of tea. "I never agreed to work evenings anyway! What a load of bollocks! I thought I was going to be involved in a normal business, not running spiritual seances."

Pavel's voice was sounding increasingly uncertain, but not because he suspected he might be in the wrong. There was just something inherently defeatist about this monologue. He was in that kind of mood. Pavel found his jeans and got dressed as though he were on his way to the dentist. Running through a succession of mildly aggressive speeches for the defence in his head, he suddenly realized with genuine vexation that what he'd actually expected from this job had been something completely different. He'd effectively thrown himself from a cliff into the sea, in an attempt to destroy everything that was hurting, everything connected with Natasha. The way novocaine blocks the synapses and numbs the pain. (It occurred to him that there was even something sweetly murderous in the word itself: novo-Cain.) But he'd simply landed in shallow water and was sitting there pathetically, rubbing his injured side.

Maybe it wasn't Maxim's fault after all.

Pavel couldn't explain why, but he felt as though he were approaching his own execution. He was so reluctant to even enter the building that he had to physically force himself over the threshold.

At first Pavel was greeted with good humour. As soon as he saw him Maxim broke into a charming smile and, winking at Elya, quoted a line from a popular cartoon, the essence of which was "we rescued him from the rubbish tip, and now he thinks he's too good for us". Although the meaning of the joke wasn't exactly reassuring, the light-hearted delivery had to count for something.

"Elya, sweetheart, why don't you pop out for a bit? Take an extra hour before lunch. You could have a little look round the shops."

Right then, Pavel knew that it was bad. Very bad.

Elya understood too, somehow, and hurriedly got ready to leave, though she couldn't resist joking about the possibility of a pay rise on her way out, seeing as Maxim had mentioned the shops.

Maxim sat there in silence. He still wore the same expression, which might have been sarcastic, it was impossible to know for sure, but Pavel felt very uneasy: so many masks.

Maxim just sat there, saying nothing. His expression didn't change. He might have been mocking him with his eyes, Pavel couldn't tell, but he began to feel very uneasy: so many masks.

"What exactly are you playing at, you little shit?" Maxim began quietly.

"Look, I'm sorry, I just..."

"You just what? You just thought you'd bunk off on a date? Romance in the air, couldn't help yourself, was that it? Or did you think this was some kind of dating agency? You didn't get the wrong door did you, by any chance?"

Pavel was rooted to the spot. He couldn't get over the vitriol, the thuggish way in which his second cousin was hissing these words at him through his teeth.

"Why, what happened?" was all he could mutter, like an idiot.

"What happened? You happened, you stupid bastard! I only had my balls twisted by the security staff of our esteemed Mr Lvov, that's all! Then I had a phone call from our esteemed Mr Lvov himself. 'Where's my daughter?' he wanted to know." Maxim had broken into a theatrical falsetto, and Pavel froze. "Well, if you must know, I saw your darling daughter disappear with one of my employees, who had the fucking nerve to reject my calls all evening! Yes, I'm afraid your darling daughter went off with a junior clerk from ARTavia! The upshot, my dear chap, is that if her father decides to get angry, as well as ramming his gold card – which, incidentally, is worth ten times your salary, even ten times mine – up our arses he'll probably get rid of us for good. Do you understand? Do you have even the faintest idea of what I'm talking about?"

Pavel was starting to get the picture. He blinked and opened his mouth, feebly trying to string a sentence together.

"Oh, just fuck off," concluded Maxim, his voice suddenly flat and emotionless. He stared pointedly at his computer screen. "I don't need people like you here."

It took Pavel forever to leave the freakish monstrosity of the business centre. It was like fighting his way out of the wreckage of a collapsed building. First he had to wait ages for the lift, then he had to navigate various reconstruction and repair sites. Struggling for breath, he loosened the knot of his tie. Death of a salesman, ha. (He gave a faint smile.) The combination of the thick blue glass and the gloomy weather made everything look inhumanly bleak and dreary. Finally stumbling outside, he looked around and wondered what to do with himself. A crooked column of vehicles were thundering down the main street, some clearing up the remnants of dirty snow after others. If a car happened to be parked at the side of the road, the snow-sweepers drove round it, briefly disrupting their relentless progress. It didn't really matter what he did now, did it?

He set off down the main street, trying to think straight, to suppress this nervous prickling sensation, at the same time absurdly preoccupied with the idea that he might bump into Elya. What would he say to her apart from, "You can have my mug"? Some workers were changing the poster high up on an advertising hoarding. The construction cradle was shaking from their exertions, and the snow beneath them looked like a murder site: torn scraps of paper, worn out rags, scattered cloths.

Fair enough. It was no more than he deserved. In fact a clean break was probably for the best, though it didn't stop him burning with humiliation. Pavel walked along feeling like a reject, his throat still trembling from Maxim's thuggish attitude and pseudo-prison slang – not out of fear, but loathing. Loathing that was at least partly directed at his own pathetic, stuttering self.

He should have walked out earlier, on his own terms. On the other hand, maybe he'd needed this blow to the head to finally knock the blinkers from his eyes. Pavel trudged through the snow, cursing himself aloud as he blindly followed a battered bus, the last surviving specimen of the Icarus brand. Christ, what had he got himself into? Who had he got involved with? And why had he got involved with them in the first place? It turned out that ARTavia were just a bunch of con artists – maybe more convincing than most, with their network of feeding troughs and lucrative estates operating in all the major cities, thanks to inspired pretenders like Maxim. But it could have been worse. When Natasha left – and he should have stopped her, or gone with her – he had panicked and grabbed whatever lay within reach. At least they were only con artists and not assassins! He would have agreed to anything at the time. Maybe even taken on the role of lookout while someone was being suffocated, clawing at the carpet with his nails. He didn't care. At least, not back then. Pavel's head was clearer now.

But it wasn't even about that. There was no moral to this story. What did morals have to do with it?

Nothing had come of any of it. Everything that he had tried to do, in the depths of his despair, had been in vain: he was no better off than before. Pavel's desperation filled him with rage.

He wanted to punch Maxim, the smug bastard.

To beat the living daylights out of him.

He didn't give a shit about anything else.

Pavel spent the rest of the day wandering round the city. He could still remember the steps that led into the underground passage from his childhood, because towards the end of winter they went from being merely slippery to being deadly, and it was a miracle that more people didn't break their necks. The steps were the red-brown colour of blood, the most prosaic kind of granite in the USSR. When he was younger they had reminded him of meat, which was a deficit commodity at the time: the bits that were dirty white and trampled were like layers of fat, bones or gristle, depending on the type of snow. As he walked beneath the dull underground lamps Pavel also remembered being strangely convinced when he was younger that cars didn't really drive overhead. He knew that was the point of underground passages, of course, but believed that it was merely theoretical. It was funny to imagine feeling that way now. Back then the adult world appeared to be so full of formalities, most of which were useless mirages, and it was almost impossible to believe that people would actually choose to go underground just so that they could walk beneath cars.

On the other hand, it was hard to ignore the evidence. Pavel could feel the shudders caused by heavy lorries and trams running up and down the middle of the main street, even now. A year ago they had taken the tracks up and replaced them with Czech technology, using some kind of special rubber to reduce the noise, which had given rise to a number of enthusiastic reports in the local press. Recently some of the inhabitants of the buildings that lined the street had written to the same newspapers, asking why the trams were no quieter. In response, a city bureaucrat had explained that this would have meant buying special (presumably Czech) carriages too.

Now Pavel was walking past an endlessly long building, apparently some kind of hostel. A series of identical irons were visible in the lower windows, their non-ferrous soles identically reflecting the non-ferrous world. He wanted to prove to Natasha that he wasn't just a waste of space either, that he was also ambitious and determined. But that was just wishful thinking. At the end of the day, he was who he was, with all his failures, accomplishments, pluses and minuses. Of course Natasha had never actually told him that he was a waste of space, but... He was not necessarily an art expert in Olga's eyes, but at least she saw him as someone capable of thoughts and feelings, someone with his own views and opinions. Olga was interested in his opinions. That much was obvious. Why the hell should he force himself to be somebody he wasn't?

He had an unexpected phone call that evening, from his former boss. Maxim's voice was calm, concentrated.

"Pavel, just make sure you avoid any more cosy little chats with Olga Evgenievna Lvova, okay? You're a big boy now. I shouldn't need to spell it out for you. It just causes problems for the company. Got it?"

"Yes."

"If you want to hand your notice in, you're free to go off with whoever you like, whenever you like."

So he hadn't been fired then. Not that it made any difference.

"What's the matter with you?" asked Igor, when Pavel arrived at Danil's place.

"What do you mean?"

"You look all... stressed out."

Strange that he could tell just by looking at him.

Danil was surrounded by stacks of heavy books bound in velvet: old issues of the magazine *Ogonek* that his deceased grandfather had kept and filed away half a century ago. They had been unearthed recently somewhere in the depths of the apartment, which by contemporary standards featured an unusual number of store-rooms.

The magazines were a visual feast! The colours used to illustrate the covers and insets were mesmerizing. One particularly charming example of this was a peach-toned portrait of Mao. And then there were the issues from 1962, featuring portraits of the cosmonauts. You could sense the magical aura of the year those exceptional individuals had appeared in Russia: adored by all, young, good-looking and apparently perfect in every way, with unfeasibly impeccable biographies and unfeasibly enhanced smiles. Like gods descended from Olympus.

While Danil talked excitedly, with barely concealed enthusiasm, about his discovery and how interesting it all was, Pavel tried to work out whether or not he meant it. It seemed that poor Danil simply didn't seem to know how to occupy himself, how to take his mind off things.

Poor Danil sensed that Pavel was distracted as he leafed through the glossy pages, pausing a little at anything to do with architecture.

"I might try and sell them," he added uncertainly. "They're probably worth quite a bit."

"You reckon?"

The rarest issues – those dating from March 1953, with imposing cover images of the late Stalin – were unfortunately not in any condition to sell, because someone (presumably

Danil's grandfather) had gone through all the articles, including the accounts of Stalin's funeral, and violently scratched out every single reference to Beria. Every mention of his name, every image, every speech.

They sat down at the table with a few beers.

"So what's happened?" Igor asked again.

Pavel didn't know where to start. "I got fired," would have been the most effective answer but was no longer appropriate, as – technically, at least – it wasn't true. Instead he needed to find the words to explain that a line had been crossed and things could no longer go back to the way they were before.

Pavel gathered his thoughts. He probably ought to start at the beginning.

"I met a girl... A really interesting girl, actually. Her name's Olga."

"Ah, I see!"

At first he didn't understand his friends' enthusiastic response to this news. Or rather, he didn't pay much attention to the torrent of macho banter that was unleashed: Igor was practically winking at him with both eyes simultaneously, and Danil made a point of telling an old joke about a biker, who had "masturbated in the shower so many times that he got an erection whenever it started raining." The message was loud and clear, and they had already started reinforcing it with comments such as "Good for you!" and "About time too!" When Pavel finally realized what was going on, he was hurt. The jokes were just a front for something more depressing: as far as his friends were concerned, Natasha had dumped him. As far as his friends were concerned, she could go to hell. They were keen for him to move on. They wanted revenge.

"All right, you two!" interrupted Pavel, as firmly as he could. "I'm being serious." And then he started talking. He talked for a long time, about everything. About the argument with Maxim and the evening he'd spent with Olga. About everything that had led up to it, what it was like working at ARTavia, what the company was all about, what he'd seen and what he'd heard over the past two months. About the smug, self-satisfied face that was just asking to be punched.

They listened in silence, sipping their beer. His words obviously made an impression on them. Danil joked that it was like Putin's provocative "Munich speech", a phrase that was common currency at the time following the Russian president's widely publicized attack on US foreign policy. After a while Igor started to pace about the kitchen. He didn't even seem to be listening properly. Preoccupied, tense and dishevelled, he wore an agitated, even slightly maniacal expression. Every now and then it looked as though he were about to overturn his stool.

"It's too much!" he suddenly exclaimed, his eyebrows raised in apparent delight at this revelation. "They're going to keep interfering in your personal life, deciding who you are and aren't allowed to see... They're going to ruin everything for you!"

This unnerved Pavel and he started to object, his voice betraying his hesitation. "Hang on, what's my personal life got to do with it? I mean, of course... But it wasn't like that..."

"Relax!" Danil jokingly raised his hand, like an image from a Soviet poster. He seemed to have perked up a bit, as though he could finally feel solid ground beneath his feet after the uncertainty of the past few days. "Seriously, what's the big deal? It was just a date. Nobody died!"

"It wasn't a date," Pavel protested weakly, but Igor interrupted him.

"They're completely taking the piss! Calling themselves an airline, going round issuing gold cards... Gold cards, my arse! It's all lies. They're robbing people blind and raking in the cash. It's just a massive, well-orchestrated scam. Don't you remember what those pilots said in Moscow?"

Of course, in the interest of fairness it was worth pointing out that the half-drunken horror stories they'd heard in the hostel had been wildly overstated for maximum effect and were therefore best taken with more than a grain of salt. Like fishermen describing "the one that got away", the pilots had been metaphorically holding their hands apart in mid-air to illustrate the holes in the fuselage. Despite the exaggerations, however, their tales were a little too close to the truth. And in any case, he didn't feel like objecting. They were all caught up in the almost forgotten euphoria of camaraderie. After the shocks he'd experienced that day, Pavel was overflowing with unexpected joy.

"You shouldn't put up with it!" declared Igor, interrupting his pacing in order to sip his beer. "You need to fight back. If they try to control you again, you should tell them where to stick their job! Do you really need it that badly?"

"Fuck them!" cried Pavel, suddenly fearless. "It's basically fraud, and I don't want anything more to do with it. I'm a law-abiding citizen!"

Oddly enough, in all the time he'd been working at that damned airline it was the first time he'd seriously thought about it. About the fact that tomorrow this heap of non-ferrous scrap, bought over the border on the cheap, really could crash. And people would die. People whose membership cards he, Pavel, had personally processed. People he'd mollified with all those fairy tales about "complete and absolute safety". Then what? Would he end up with blood on his hands for his part in it all?

What if someone he cared about boarded one of these planes?

He immediately thought of Natasha, as usual, but she was a long way away. She was safe. What about Olga, though? He had filled out her registration forms himself. What if she were to fly?

"No, we're not going to stand for it. We'll fight the bastards!" Danil suddenly declared, slapping the table. "Are we in this together, or not?"

They looked at one another and magic hovered in the kitchen, which was full of winter silence and oily light spots that fell into the discoloured sink, casting shadows onto the ancient plastic of the portable radio and various culinary syringes. The smell of adventure was in the air. The smell of something crazy, something new, something young and frivolous, after a long, boring hibernation.

They all felt like blowing up this unbearable life – the way a hungry bear destroys its den on waking, scattering the earth with its body more forcefully than any grenade.

Pavel was at the end of his tether, because he no longer had an outlet for the pain of rejection and the wounded pride that had been building up inside him. Should he channel it into destroying everything around him?

Danil was at the end of his tether, because he could no longer pretend that he couldn't hear the whispering behind his back: "the monster". Like the effects of fatigue on steel cables. He was an emotional wreck. He hadn't done anything wrong, and even if he had then he had atoned for it a long time ago. Still, it bothered him. Rebellion was the only option left.

As for Igor, he threw himself into this new adventure with the hungry enthusiasm of a writer. He was the same every time a project captured his imagination. Like a new book? In a way, except Igor had begun to understand that he was never going to have any success with real books.

So he threw himself even more zealously into real life: he began to write life itself, and he found this considerably more exciting.

Agatha Christie once wrote about an old theatre actor who was called upon to investigate a murder. At some point in the past this actor had played the role of a lame detective, and as soon as he started to think about the murder, to try and get to the bottom of it, he developed a slight limp. He had slipped back into character, without even realizing it.

The three friends sat in the kitchen late into the night, while the TV stayed on in the abandoned living room. A beer advert filled the screen. According to a new law alcohol adverts were no longer allowed to feature people, so the brand managers and marketing teams had to take a more creative approach. This nocturnal world varied enormously, but it was so strange without people. A strange, strange world.

CHAPTER 10

Pavel was amused by the idea of himself as a film critic. Over the past few days he and Olga had exchanged four or five emails, discussing old films so seriously that he'd resorted to furtively delving into Wikipedia. Being an expert required certain sacrifices.

A row of turnstiles stood at the entrance to the lobby, their red eyes glowing, and several minions wearing black uniform were checking people's passes, nodding everyone through. More deadly seriousness. There wasn't a lot of logic in this zealous regime, because there were so many different companies in the building that the security staff were subject to a constant stream of different passes, permits and business cards. It was the start of the working day and a kind of human dam was forming inside the doors. This watery expression was particularly apt given the way the snow was coming down in big, damp flakes. Some people had been smart enough to bring umbrellas and shook them as they came inside, spraying wet snow everywhere. Women moaned about their ruined make-up, and everyone was swarming and humming with discontent in the damp, overcrowded foyer. Meanwhile the blizzard surrounded the building, swirling about the dark blue glass.

"ARTavia," Pavel said clearly, presenting his card as nonchalantly as he could. The security guard nodded. The way was open.

It was funny to think that he was putting himself in jeopardy right now. Pavel stepped into the lift and was enfolded by wet raincoats; the catch of office plankton was hauled upwards, water splashing from the net. He was enjoying the frisson of danger that came with being a spy, a sleuth, whatever he was, on a mission. Pavel had a secret memory stick in his pocket, and no one was supposed to know about it.

Initially, their brainstorming session in Danil's apartment on "how to fight the sect" (for that was how they now referred to the airline) was not particularly productive. They were unable to come up with a workable plan of attack, so the council of war dragged on. As a proud "contributor to the regional newspaper", Igor explained that getting the press involved was not an option – not because of the number of high-placed friends (or clients) ARTavia had in the city, or because everything had already been "taken care of", but simply because there was nothing the local press could do. They were perfectly happy to stick to running stories on officially approved matters (including court cases), referring to "businessman R", "company N", and so on to cover themselves. Official censorship and phone calls from junior bureaucrats were no longer necessary, since they automatically conformed.

"We sit in the editorial office, spread our hands and say to everyone, 'There's nothing we can do, you know how it is, would you like some tea?'" explained Igor, spreading his fingers. "And that's all I can say to you – I mean, to us: there's nothing we can do. Pah! I'm sick of living like this."

As it happened, they were helped by the press after all – but by a different newspaper, and in a different way. They were helped by the publication of a certain article in *The Times*. (Gosh, that sounds so civilized! It makes you want to sit by the fire and smoke a pipe.) To be more precise, by the translation of an article from *The Times* that appeared on the Russian mass media website *inoSMI*, which was inordinately popular at the time. Maxim crowed triumphantly as soon as he came across it in the labyrinthine depths of the internet. He didn't collect these articles and file them away in his red folder for nothing! The folder was often taken to the Avant-Garde House of Culture or to other venues where "friends of the company" were meeting. The articles were often photocopied and distributed, with dark margins either side of the text like an art house film. The articles often helped. ARTavia loved impressionable people. But this particular English article was the pearl of the collection, and for that reason it is worth replicating in full:

A Turbulent Echo of the Past

The Tupolev aircraft that fly over Russia and China are capable of inspiring terror even before take-off. There is something more than a little disconcerting about the way the flight attendants conduct the pre-flight safety briefing, instructing passengers to use the escape ropes in the event of an emergency.

Flight engineers walk up and down the aisle brandishing spanners, and during the final preparations before take-off they use them forcefully to beat the panel upholstery back into place.

As soon as the plane takes off they disappear into the toilets, often accompanied by the prim flight attendants, and cigarette smoke can be seen escaping from beneath the toilet door for the entire duration of the flight. Meanwhile the passengers do their best to shelter from the jets of freezing air that penetrate the aircraft through gaps surrounding the poorly adjusted safety hatches.

The regularity with which alcoholic drinks are taken into the cockpit arouses a certain apprehension, but at least this explains the aeroplane's sudden bursts of speed. Tupolevs do not have a cruise control system, so when the pilot decides to put his foot down he forces his passengers back into their seats.

It goes without saying that the in-flight dining experience is as traumatic as being jolted about roughly in the air for 12 hours straight. Fidel Castro once joked that flying with Aeroflot was as much of a threat to his life as the CIA, and it's not hard to see why.

The lamentable condition of the aircraft used on domestic routes during the Soviet era was reflected in the NATO code names they were given: the Tu-134, which was originally modelled on a strategic bomber and even has a glass nose to accommodate the gunner, was known as 'Crusty', and the Tu-154 was labelled 'Careless'.

Justifying this nickname, the crew of a Tu-154

forgot to lower the landing gear on approach to a Greek airport in 2000, and the plane skidded along the landing strip on its undercarriage before taking off again and going around prior to a second attempt at landing.

"Brilliant, isn't it?" grinned Maxim. He was looking at Pavel expectantly, wanting him to share his amusement. He had spent the past few days trying to pretend that their argument had never happened. Pavel wasn't interested in going along with this charade. He couldn't have laughed at the paranoid Brits now even if he'd wanted to.

"The 'cruise control' thing's a bit over the top, of course," continued Maxim, without waiting for a reaction. "Such nervous gentlemen they have working at *The Times*!"

There were plenty of nervous gentlemen (and ladies, of course) closer to home as well. You only had to look at ARTavia's client database to see just how many, and all willing to give out their email addresses. Let them soothe their souls, their stomachs, their sphincter muscles, whatever they clenched in fear. Let them read once more about the deplorable state of the aviation industry, and then let them thank God for the existence of a company whose aircraft would never crash, as everyone knew, because they were governed by exceptional karma, and so on and so forth, according to the mantra.

"Elya, please send this out as an attachment to everyone on the mailing list."

Although Pavel feigned ambivalence while they were discussing the article, he was fascinated by one particular aspect of it. Namely, the astonishing, deeply entrenched arrogance of the company's management, which seemed almost to be verging on naivety. After all, if you ignored the livery (the company branding on the sides of the aircraft), and if you thought about the creaking and groaning that went on when the aircraft was straining to take off, then the article could have been written about ARTavia! Old Tupolev planes bought on the black market in Central Asia, drunk and hungover crews on meagre salaries... Only a blind person could fail to spot the similarities. Which is effectively what these wealthy locals, with the glamorous word "aerophobia" in their files, were.

"They send them the article and Maxim somehow manages to turn it to their advantage, basically saying, 'Look at us, while this nightmare's going on around us we're as pure as the driven snow'," ranted Pavel. "You've got to admit, it takes a certain talent. What a bastard!"

"But what if... What if everyone on the mailing list received a follow-up email after the article? Something like, 'What you have just read applies directly and above all to the airline ARTavia itself.' We could quote a few facts and figures, mention how old their planes are and the fact that they come from... where? Turkmenistan?"

"Kazakhstan."

"Same difference. Kazakhstan, then. We can easily set up a fake email account, though we'll have to register it at an internet café so they can't trace the IP."

It was easy enough to clarify the Kazakhstan connection – and a lot more besides. Danil spent several days surfing the internet, and the first thing that became clear was that they weren't the first to speak up against the corporation. In the depths of various online forums he managed to uncover detailed reports, quotes and scraps of evidence relating to ARTavia's activity in different regions. There were also signs that someone had tracked and removed this data, or at least that they had attempted to do so. Secondly, he managed to piece together a few facts and figures: when and where individual aircraft had been bought, in what condition, what incidents they had been involved in, and so on. This involved typing the aircraft registration numbers into search engines and the tedious, tedious job of sifting through the results. There wasn't much data available yet, but it could still be put to good use. They managed to pull it together into a kind of database, which would make enlightening reading for the gullible "friends of the company".

Pavel knew from the outset that it was not going to be easy to complete the mission. A few days previously Elya had been rushing between her exams and medical treatments, turning up at work occasionally, but more often phoning in to make her excuses and ask favours. During one of her absences Pavel had been required to log into her computer to send something urgent to the printer. It was just him and Maxim in the office, and the tense silence was becoming more and more oppressive. Pavel couldn't bring himself to lighten the atmosphere, even with a joke. Elya had come in today, albeit reluctantly, and she was going to be there for some time because she had to deal with some overdue financial reports. So it was going to be difficult to sneak onto her computer, which was where the list of clients and their email addresses were stored, and he couldn't think of a legitimate reason to access it. Pavel rearranged the pencils on his desk and racked his brains. Could he openly ask her to send him the database on some pretext or other? No, that wouldn't work...

He would just have to bide his time until Elya left the office, and it would help if Maxim chose the same moment to absent himself as well. In other words, a rather specific set of circumstances was required.

But the day was characterized by routine and rainy

windows, and nothing out of the ordinary happened, with the exception of the sudden and brief appearance of Danil. First, Pavel's phone rang.

"Hi, listen, do you know if there's anywhere near you I can photocopy a passport?" Danil asked hurriedly. "It's urgent."

"No... I don't know..." said Pavel, struggling to think straight. "Hang on, just come here! We've got a photocopier."

"Seriously?"

"Yeah, no problem. Just be careful when you come in, the security checks are a bit full-on at the moment."

Danil arrived almost immediately. He wasn't wearing a hat, and his long hair hung in fat, wet snakes. They met in the lobby and slapped each other on the back, then stood waiting for the lift.

"So, this is where the evil empire's based, then?"

"Keep your voice down!"

Danil needed to photocopy his entire passport, from the first page to the last, and while Pavel got on with it Elya entertained their visitor, even flirting with him a little. When they'd finished Danil glanced at his watch. "Damn, I've missed it... The solicitor's office is closed for lunch. I'll have to find somewhere to wait until they open."

Pavel didn't ask any questions. He'd heard something about Danil's grandmother signing the apartment over, transferring the deeds, and so on, but he didn't get involved in other peoples' business.

"There's a little café upstairs. Do you want to grab a coffee?"

They sat there apathetically with their plastic cups and little stirring sticks, looking out at the dark city that was swimming in red lights. Pavel lazily flicked through the pages of Danil's passport. Passports tend to be more or less identical, but Pavel didn't have this one: a fat stamp (even the letters had started to run) under the elegantly composed heading "Military Service".

"Are you jealous?" asked Danil, with a rueful smile.

"I'm not sure."

This stamp was put in the passports of those who were exempt from conscription (though still eligible for universal mobilization in the event of war, which was an unlikely eventuality), or those who had already completed their military service. Or those who had already turned twenty-seven. Or...

It was this final, ambiguous "or" that applied to Danil, and Pavel completely understood why his friend was smiling so sadly. Various different stories had circulated over the years. While they were still at university it was common knowledge that Danil had been exempted from military service, without even trying to get out of it. The official explanation related to his grandmother's disability category, to her guardianship of Danil and other mitigating circumstances. The unofficial version, of course, referred to the Cheboksary incident. There was an assumption that the psychiatrist at the military enlistment office had immediately struck his name off the list as soon as he opened his file. Unfortunately, this was probably not too far from the truth. Unfortunately, this also explained Danil's mood and the way he said, "I don't even envy myself. Why should you?"

"This'll make you laugh... I had a dream the other night..."

Pavel couldn't quite remember the dream itself, as is often the case. All that remained were a handful of images, like fragments of an old film where the picture barely moves. (In Pavel's early childhood their local cinema had been closed down to make way for a shop, then another, but for a long time there had been scraps of film scattered about, coloured and black and white; Pavel and his friends had gathered them up and tried to put them back together, to find out what was on them, to make out the pictures.) All that remained was the feeling.

Pavel could vaguely remember that the dream was about him leaving for the army, and he seemed to be happy about it – at least, he was looking forward to something new. The dream itself was defined by the sense of something new, which was conveyed in exquisitely subtle ways. The anticipation of change, new friendships, a different life.

Random episodes from his dream swam to the surface, not actually directly related to the army. In one of them Pavel was waiting to be assigned to a unit after appearing before the conscription commission, but for some reason he was in an apartment. (Who else was there?) And he had that horrible feeling that you get in dreams, as though you're late, or you've missed something, or forgotten something – it's agonizing. In one of the more amusing parts of the dream Pavel was doing push-ups in the shadowy apartment to avoid making a fool of himself on the parade-ground in front of everyone, but then he was suddenly out on the parade-ground and he was too tired to do any more push-ups, and everyone was laughing at him, but in a good way. So there must have been a parade-ground, after all.

This stupid dream had subsequently reminded him of something else, in the way it had made him feel. A long time ago, just as the previous century was coming to the end of its trajectory and Yeltsin was serving out his final term in office, a comedy film called *Demobbed* had come out. Many Russian films like this were being made at the time, just for the fun of it – on a shoestring budget, purely for entertainment value, without burdening themselves with the fashionable term "art house" or disappearing up their own backsides.

This idiotic but calmly philosophical tale about a group of friends who are called up into the army was a revelation for Pavel and his classmates. Brought up on news reports from Chechnya and articles about the brutality of bullying in the army, they had been protected from this institution more than from death (from the moment they were born, in the shadow of the Soviet war in Afghanistan). To them it was an alien planet, and they had never even imagined that life might exist there too. Of course they realized that it was just a film, and that all the fun and excitement existed only on screen, but still it opened their eyes to the possibility that there might be something out there, "on the other side" – in the afterlife, as they had been brought up to believe. Maybe they were missing out on something! Of course, no one rushed to the military enlistment office – when the time came, they rushed to university instead – and this fleeting feeling dissipated that very evening, as they pensively sipped bitter foam from cans of beer. Pavel had forgotten all about it until now, years later, when the dream reminded him. Once he'd remembered, he thought about it some more.

Naturally, having managed to evade conscription themselves, they weren't in any position to judge how and to what extent things had changed in real terms. Pavel could only evaluate how the attitude to conscription had changed amongst those who were younger than them, even if only by three years. No one was exactly desperate to go, so in that respect nothing had changed. But it was no longer the ultimate ordeal, to be fought against tooth and nail. Someone he knew who had got married young – evidently it hadn't quite worked out – went off to sign up with thinly disguised relief. Someone else had a friend who was killed in a car accident, and for some reason he decided that he had to go and do his military service. There were some very creative send-offs, too: the ceremonial shaving of heads by a group of friends, everyone taking photos, hundreds of images uploaded to social networking sites.

In the end, it wasn't a matter of personal choice. No one pretended otherwise. But still... They left without making a fuss. They stayed in touch online. They lived. They came back. Their worlds were not turned upside down.

It was so different to the way it had been for Pavel's generation, to the fear that had been instilled in them from early childhood. His mother had an energetic friend called Galina Borisovna, who was a teacher. When she gave birth to her son, who was the same age as Pavel, not only did she fail to treat his psoriasis – she actually sought to exacerbate it (or so it seemed). She kept all paperwork relating to his condition for future medical commissions. While her son was practically still a baby she declared that she would not be giving him to the army, even though it wouldn't come looking for him until the following century.

People's entire lives were dedicated to avoiding the army. Some people's parents arranged official medical diagnoses, such as schizophrenia, which hung over them forever. Some were pushed into the sciences, along the university-postgraduate-PhD route, and this also affected the rest of their lives. Only later, once they'd grown up, did they really start to think about it and to ask themselves whether it had all been worth it.

Pavel was thinking about it now. It still seemed as though life were only just beginning, that these were the preliminary years and they just had to be patient, to wait a little longer. But this was life. Not the start of life, but life itself – and it wasn't going well. What was it all for?

Depressing thoughts. Depressing conversations. It must have been the weather. The city had been engulfed in a terrible blizzard, and the dark blue windows made it impossible to tell whether dusk had fallen.

"I have to go," said Danil. He stood up, crumpling his plastic cup.

"Make sure you don't get it wet. Have you got anything to put it in, like a folder or a carrier bag?"

Pavel went back down to his floor. Nothing was going right today.

The night before he'd had an unusually long and subdued conversation with Natasha. It was daytime in Pittsburgh. She hadn't gone to her lessons. She didn't really explain or tell him what was wrong, but she was in a bad mood right from the start of their Skype chat. Not even a bad mood, as such – she just seemed apathetic, reserved and unhappy. Then she started crying. Pavel gently consoled her, though he genuinely didn't know what to say. He faltered and fell silent, but his heart was aching. It wasn't as though they hadn't been open with each other before, but... Up until now he had been obsessed with the idea that she'd gone off and left him, that she didn't care about him, that he meant nothing to her. He had been too busy licking his own wounds. Now he was overwhelmed with compassion when he thought about her out there on her own, exhausted and lonely – she'd headed off into the unknown without thinking it through, and she was finding it a lot harder than she had imagined. It was all so different. Pavel thought about his feelings, as though he were running his fingers over his (heart)-strings. Particularly since he'd got to know Olga (hadn't he?) and found himself thinking about her more and more, since he'd let himself get carried away (hadn't he?), he... Logically, he ought to break up with Natasha. It wouldn't be the end of the world. They'd been through bad patches before. But right now, he was surprised by the tenderness of his feelings for her.

"Hang in there," he said into the microphone, with surprising solemnity. "You're strong. And so am I."

CHAPTER 11

"We're meeting at seven," said Igor. There was the sound of horns in the background, as though he were swinging through the city jungle from vine to vine. "What does she drink?"

"Who?" asked Pavel, confused.

"Pavel, do try not to behave like a complete moron," chided Igor, with fake annoyance. Suddenly his tone changed. "Hang on, you did invite her, didn't you?"

"Of course," said Pavel, frowning in exasperation.

"Right then, shall I get some wine? I hope she won't be expecting Veuve Clicquot. Will a Black Sea vintage do?"

He'd had the most ridiculous start to the weekend. His parents had woken up early and, with much shouting and swearing, liberated the balcony of an unruly perennial. There were some vegetables cooking in the kitchen, and the windows were covered with condensation so thick that you could make out the individual drops against the grey of the sky. It was like a Wilson cloud chamber. And now Igor was doing his head in. Pavel still didn't understand the point of a general gathering of their anti-ARTavia "partisan detachment", let alone why they had to invite Olga, but Igor had insisted. So Pavel had caved in and dialled her number with fumbling fingers, then stumbled over his words. It was never a good idea to put Igor in charge: you ended up getting sucked into his scenarios and were unable to break free, as though you were trapped in some kind of hallucination. Pavel had noticed this before. But there was something else too, something more mundane: his friends were keen to see Olga for themselves, to welcome her "into the family". They had made such a fuss about inviting her that Pavel couldn't help questioning their motives. To spite "Natasha the traitor", anyone would do. Ah, he's met a girl, has he? Excellent. Now, moving on...

Or maybe he was reading too much into it. He prowled through the gloomy day like a caged animal, reluctantly helping with the household chores. He took the doormats down to the courtyard and laid them on the untouched snow in one of the corners, which was miraculously untouched. The snow was damp and yielded readily.

Olga accepted the invitation enthusiastically.

"Oh, what's the occasion? Should I bring anything?"

Like what, Veuve Clicquot? At least she didn't ask what she should wear.

Suddenly animated, she announced that she would arrive from Red Springs at 8 p.m. She would take a taxi to Danil's address, which she had written down carefully, so no one needed to come out and meet her.

"Eight o'clock? That's too late," grumbled Igor. "Call her back! Tell her to come earlier."

But it was already out of Pavel's hands.

"What if I come earlier instead, will that be okey?"

He really didn't like hanging out at Danil's place. The lampshades, which dated back to the Brezhnev era, were so dusty and stained with old age that they looked more like marble than glass. The dodgy wiring was even older. Whatever the reason, it was always dark there. As soon as the sun took cover – and in winter it disappeared like illicit cargo, in the blink of an eye – the room was covered in a drowsy veil.

Danil wasn't there when Pavel arrived. Igor explained importantly that he'd gone to the shop to buy some foreign cheese. And olives. A strategic supply of red wine was already waiting on the cold windowsill, the necks of the bottles showing up black, like warheads.

"One each?" winked Igor.

Pavel barely acknowledged him with a nod. As if it wasn't bad enough already, now they were planning a full-on drinking session in front of Olga. They were bound to drink too much and scare her off, then try to kiss her goodbye with wine-stained lips. Or try something else.

Igor began reading aloud from a newspaper, like a radio announcer. "'Soviet cosmonaut Valentina Tereshkova, who is about to celebrate a significant birthday, opens up in a rare interview in Star City.'" He shook the newspaper and continued. "There are some great quotes here! Check this out... Talking about space tourists, she says she'd go herself if she had the money!"

"Good for her. How old is she now?"

"They don't say which birthday it is. Her seventieth, probably. Never mind that, listen to this bit about Mars: 'My hobby is the incredible, enigmatic Red Planet, which Sergei Pavlovich Korolyev and I dreamed about several decades ago.'"

"Well, it's good to keep dreaming," remarked Pavel. He uncorked one of the bottles, after removing the foil with a fork, and thought that if Natasha hadn't decided to go off to the States she would have been obsessed with the idea for the rest of her life. It would have eaten her up, and him as well.

"That's not even the best bit. Listen... 'I would gladly fly there and never come back.' Can you believe that?"

"What?"

"That's what she said! It's like... I don't know. I thought up a great story about it – in fact, I might even write it down. It's like this massive dystopia, where iconic images of the past are fundamentally incompatible with modern life and it's unrealistic for them to even carry on existing, you know? Anyway, my story's about Tereshkova being sent to Mars, at her own request, as part of her seventieth birthday celebrations. The launch is broadcast live on TV, it's all over the press, and the whole nation is rejoicing. Like it's all perfectly normal. I'm calling it 'Tereshkova: Mission to Mars'. The main character is a journalist who accompanies her through the preparations, chatting with her, spending time with her. It's like they're preparing for the launch together."

Igor spoke with such enthusiasm, and his eyes shone with such confidence, that for the first time Pavel was struck by the idea that maybe, one day, his roller-coaster of crazy ideas might actually lead somewhere.

"You know, it would be better to set it ten years ago, in 1997," suggested Pavel, with sudden sincerity. "Make it her sixtieth birthday."

"Why?" asked Igor, surprised.

"Because it would make more sense. The 1990s were all about getting rid of everything connected with the past, including the iconic images that represented it. This fantasy of yours definitely belongs in that era. Things are different now."

"Do you really think so?" asked Igor, with a sceptical smile.

Pavel was actually thinking about something completely different. Tereshkova reminded him of Natasha's mother. Anna Mikhailovna had called the day before, out of the blue. He had answered impatiently, not recognizing her voice, and she had almost hung up in fright.

"Pavel dear, I'm so sorry to disturb you... Are you in the middle of something? I've got to go to hospital tomorrow, to the cardiology department. Don't worry, it's nothing serious..."

Pavel was in the middle of a stressful situation at work (a client had lost his card, his flight was that evening and Pavel was having trouble processing his ticket), and at first he couldn't make any sense of the call. Who? What? Where was she going, and why? Anna Mikhailovna broke off, then began to assure him that everything was fine. Still distracted, Pavel thought he understood.

"Do you need help getting to the hospital? Do you have a big bag?"

"No, no, don't be silly! I'll get a taxi."

Then it occurred to Pavel that maybe she needed someone to take care of her dog, so he offered. No, the neighbours would look after the dog and her houseplants. Maybe she wanted him to tell Natasha? No, Anna Mikhailovna had already called her. He just couldn't work out what she wanted from him, but decided not to force the issue. His would-be mother-in-law became increasingly flustered, and the conversation ended awkwardly. Pavel said he hoped she'd be feeling better soon.

Once he'd finished running around, it dawned on him that Anna Mikhailovna had simply wanted to let someone know, to "check out" officially before her journey into the unknown. "So if you happen to call, don't worry if no one answers," she had said. That was hardly likely. Natasha's home life, which had been hollowed out at the core, had gradually started to fade from memory. These days his fingers would have hesitated over the telephone keypad a little longer... and a little longer still.

It made him feel sad.

Igor was quiet too, despondently sipping his dark wine. He was staring off into the corner, where a flat brush was caught up in the spider's web of an old stocking.

When Danil got back, the first thing he said was, "Ah,

you're getting a head start!" The first thing that Pavel saw was a tall, thin cone of newspaper, from which a white rose was ceremoniously extricated.

"Here, this is for you!" declared Danil, falling dramatically to one knee.

Pavel stood there, not knowing how to take the joke.

"Take the rose," grinned Igor. "Of course it's not for you. It's for Olga. When I saw that you hadn't brought any flowers, I texted Danil."

"And you owe me a hundred roubles!"

Pavel automatically prepared a heavy vase, which came to life and grew cold. The way the light was reflecting from its dull glass reminded him of a funeral. He didn't know how to react to this ridiculous pantomime; he felt confused and slightly offended.

He couldn't relax. The doorbell rang at exactly 8 p.m. The longer Pavel had been there, the more he had distanced himself from his friends – at least, as far as this was possible in a Khrushchev-era apartment. He didn't feel like talking (feeling nervous, no doubt), so sat in the kitchen in silence, hacking slices off the foreign cheese. He listened carefully to the occasional cars in the courtyard below, glancing out of the window at the strangely oversized street lamp that lived there, in its own universe of branches. About six minutes passed between the sound of the main entrance door slamming and the ring at the door to the apartment: Olga must have waited in the entrance hall until exactly 8 p.m. Was she nervous too?

Even more so. He could tell this as soon as he looked into her eyes, though naturally she entered the apartment with almost aristocratic dignity and poise. He fussed about, taking her coat. She let him. The two of them seemed to be performing a complicated dance in the tiny hallway, shuffling amongst advertising flyers stiff from dried snow, neither of them sure of the next move or able to hide their awkwardness. Igor and Danil, on the other hand greeted their guest with unprecedented enthusiasm, practically throwing themselves on her.

"Hello, Olga! Come in, don't be shy! Here, put these slippers on, I'm afraid the floor's a bit dirty."

After cracking a few more jokes about Danil's "bachelor pad", Igor led the subdued and self-conscious couple ceremoniously into the living room as though it were a registry office.

"Would you like some wine? Olga Evgenievna, do you drink red?"

"Please, call me Olga."

They sat down awkwardly, and Igor – as self-appointed host – busied himself setting out plates and glasses. It was only now that Pavel realized the stupidity of giving flowers verbally, of pointing at a rose that's already standing in a vase and saying to a guest, "That's for you!"

Sitting at the table, they clumsily raised their glasses for the first toast: "To new friends". It was a good thing they hadn't turned the TV off completely – even with the sound turned down, Pavel found it reassuring. They chatted politely about this and that, though the conversation was rather stilted. Igor held court, of course, as though it were a meeting of senior Communist Party officials. Olga held her tongue. She looked around, taking it all in. You couldn't work out – behind her aristocratic armour, behind her fixed expression – what she thought of it here, what she thought of his friends.

They really were from different worlds. There were a couple of occasions, Pavel noticed, when Olga was not exactly shocked, but certainly taken aback. For example, Igor had put little spoons out next to the can of olives that stood on the table, and Olga had been using one to carefully scoop them out – until she noticed Danil sticking his fingers straight into the brine. After this she didn't touch the olives again. Of course she didn't. (Pavel became aware of it at this point.) Why should they bother with spoons? He wanted to kick his friend under the table, but he was sitting just out of reach and decided not to risk it.

When the small talk had more or less run its course and the same was true of the snacks, they got down to business. Igor abruptly dropped his smile.

"Right then, we're here to decide what to do about ARTavia, how to take on this sect. Olga, has Pavel filled you in?"

"More or less."

"These people have built an entire empire on deceit and manipulation. What is more, their victims are rich and powerful people, and it's not only happening here. Apparently a similar scheme operates in many other regions too. It's like a network, like a..."

"Like an octopus," prompted Danil.

"Exactly. Our task is to try and cut off its tentacles, maybe even to destroy this creature completely. How much more can we take? Seriously! You read so much about that... what's he called? I've forgotten. That charlatan who claims he can bring the dead back to life, at the request of their loved ones, and for a sizeable fee. He's supposedly able to resurrect the soul of the dead person and transfer it into another body."

"You mean Grigory Grabovoy," said Olga.

"That's the one. People are always denouncing him, campaigning against him. He's in prison now, apparently, and rightly so, because he exploits those who are grieving when they're vulnerable and prepared to believe anything. He even targeted mothers of the victims of the Beslan massacre! And ARTavia are just as bad. The only difference is that they exploit people who are afraid to fly because occasionally planes crash. They also hypnotize people and use suggestion techniques."

Pavel stood up to turn the TV off, and Igor glanced at him with approval. There was something about Igor, you had to admit – he did have a certain natural charm. Although he was ungainly, overweight and generally regarded as a figure of fun, at times like this he was transformed. Even Pavel's irony retreated. When Igor's creative spark began to burn, he was a different person altogether.

Now he lowered his voice for effect.

"Please bear in mind that we're getting involved in something very dangerous. The guys at ARTavia are well connected. They've managed to hypnotize all the big shots round here, right up to the highest echelons of local government. Everyone flies with them. If we grab them by the balls (sorry, Olga) and make ourselves too visible, they'll stop at nothing to silence us."

Igor stopped talking. No one said anything. They looked at one another. Only two out of the five lamps in the living room were working (Danil's grandmother had let the light bulbs burn out, and rummaging amongst the cultural layers of the apartment for replacements would have felt like a violation). The subdued lighting made their gathering look like the Last Supper. They had drunk only a little wine, and a conspiratorial atmosphere suddenly filled the room.

Olga left at 10.30 p.m., bidding them all a warm farewell. She had thoroughly enjoyed herself. Her journey home had been carefully planned: she was going to take a taxi to the central shopping centre, where she would be met by her "father's men", as she called them. She had even called the taxi to the building next door, but that wasn't part of the plan – she'd just given the wrong address by mistake. So Pavel offered to accompany her.

They walked slowly around the building. The light from the street lamps was tinged faintly violet, and bright shadows thickened in the space between them, so that everything looked as though it were drawn in ink – diluted, undiluted.

They chatted as they walked, about nothing in particular.

As they approached the taxi Olga suddenly stopped, put her arms round him and kissed him. Then she got straight into the car. Pavel hadn't even come to his senses before the door slammed and the orange light swam slowly across the courtyard, dancing in the black windows of the ground floor.

Well! He hadn't expected that.

I bet Igor and Danil are hanging out of the window, he thought to himself, and this made him smile. Pavel's whole body was singing, and he was belatedly feeling the effects of the wine, although he didn't feel at all drunk. It was like something out of a fairytale. Pavel stood there without moving. He didn't feel like leaving straight away. He didn't feel like thinking at all.

Ahead of him in the darkness, slightly altered by their snowy hats, stood the bug-like silhouettes of three foreign cars, with light-blue diodes flashing asynchronously in their windscreens. Their alarm systems. For some reason he was reminded of a tattered and discoloured child's encyclopedia, half a century old. The volume on technology had fantasized at length about the future. The images of cars labelled "the year 2000" might indeed have looked like bugs, but the artist had imagined that they would actually fly. If someone from the 1950s were to suddenly materialize, the main thing he would notice about the cars in front of him would be the flashing blue lights: evidence of a cosmic link, or a photon engine, perhaps? Who knows what he might imagine. It would never occur to him that it was just a cheap and completely unremarkable Chinese alarm. Essentially, cars were the same as they used to be. Everything is the same as it used to be.

And the forgotten white rose remained on the windowsill.

CHAPTER 12

"Veuve Clicquot, perhaps?" suggested Maxim, pronouncing the words elegantly as he turned the bottle in his hands. It was shiny, black and smooth, like a pebble from the sea.

"What?" Pavel's heart began beating a little faster.

"No, I don't think so," said Maxim. He put the bottle back carefully and ran his finger along the display, causing a barely perceptible, vitreous movement of the air. "Or how about some Liebfraumilch? It means 'beloved woman's milk'. Do you remember how they used to translate it as 'Madonna's Milk', because the real name was too embarrassing? You haven't been drinking long enough to remember, of course."

"We tend to mix beer and vodka anyway," Pavel answered irritably. He couldn't help himself.

Maxim continued to browse the expensive imported wines, ostentatiously changing his mind. He was in top form today. Bright, spring sunshine. An excellent mood, with outbursts of cheerful garrulousness. He kept grabbing his phone, chatting animatedly and roaring with laughter. Maybe that was simply his way of warming up for the evening sermon: *Blah blah blah.*

They spent so long at the supermarket that even Elya began to lose interest, which was unusual for someone who liked shopping as much as she did. They were choosing wine and snacks for the informal buffet that almost always accompanied a gathering of ARTavia clients, or "meeting of friends", as they liked to call it. They had already been there for a good hour, which the irrepressible Maxim had spent primarily lecturing his younger colleagues on supermarket shopping techniques (items placed in the most visible locations were either expensive or close to their sell-by date; there was a whole science to it, which he'd had the opportunity to assimilate during his impetuous youth), then waving his wallet at the cashier and imperiously declaring, "Company expenses!" Pavel, pushing the trolley along gloomily behind him, felt alternately embarrassed and repulsed. He couldn't manage to shake the feeling of acute hostility that he harboured towards his boss – almost his former boss, and almost his former relative, too. It was becoming irrational in its manifestations, and Pavel even found himself enraged by qualities in Maxim that he had previously admired.

They eventually emerged into the sunlight and walked to the car park, where little streams of melting snow were already running along the edges. The way they looked, like twisted braids, reminded him of coltsfoot stems. Maxim deftly pressed a button on his key ring. The boot of his dark blue Audi clicked open.

"So, big guy, haven't you thought about getting yourself a car yet?" Maxim asked pointedly.

"No, that would be too much," Pavel retorted enigmatically, as he began throwing their purchases into the boot of the car.

"Hey, careful with those bottles!"

On top of everything, Pavel was feeling desperately sleep-deprived and could barely put one foot in front of the other. In the morning, when the sun was ready to burn through the old net curtain, which was faded on both sides, he'd got up feeling such a wreck that he'd decided to brew some coffee, which he hadn't done since his first days as a student, when lectures started unbearably early. Back then he had darted between the bathroom and the kitchen, with his toothbrush poking out of his mouth and something else threatening to poke out of his underpants, making sure that the coffee didn't boil over, watching out for the little brown hat to begin rising in the Turkish coffee pot. Back then, bursting with energy, it wasn't like he'd actually needed the caffeine. Today, feeling as old and heavy as an elephant, Pavel found the coffee first – dry and lustrous, like manganese – then the Turkish coffee pot, which was covered in greasy dust. He washed it, then decided he didn't feel like it after all.

He'd struggled to get up because he'd spent half the night talking to Natasha. She'd been in a bit of a state when she called.

"Have you heard about my mother?"

Things had been strange between them over the past few days. Previously they'd had all kinds of phone calls: affectionate ones, when she admitted that she missed him and loved him and couldn't wait to see him; and hysterical ones, when she would berate him for not calling, for not being online at the time they'd agreed... It wasn't even jealousy, more a childish kind of sulk, unfounded and merciless, her mouth clamped unattractively shut. They'd been through it all. But just lately Natasha had taken to falling silent more and more often, as though she were thinking about something that had nothing to do with Pavel. She talked, she sighed. She seemed aloof and exhausted.

"There's something wrong with her heart, isn't there?"

Of course Anna Mikhailovna herself hadn't admitted

anything so serious; she'd just spoken about medical tests, a few minor symptoms, and the spots... the spots in front of her eyes.

"I probably ought to come back," said Natasha, her voice muffled.

"Hang on a minute. What do you mean, come back? It was so hard for you to arrange the transfer."

This was so unexpected that Pavel's head was full of all kinds of conflicting thoughts. She wanted to come back now, did she? It had seemed to him that she would stop at nothing, that she would keep going on and on, always forwards, towards her radiant future, while the rest of them, her nearest and dearest... As it turned out, they were like hostages in a bad film. As it turned out, the end was in sight, and it was so mundane. There were levers after all, stopcocks and brakes. Whereas just six months previously he had been through hell precisely because there had seemed to be no way of stopping Natasha's flight.

Her mother's heart condition was serious, though. Very serious.

"Listen, maybe there's something I could do? I'm here, I could help your mother. She knows me. I could pick up her medicine, look after her, whatever she needs. Let me help... Seriously, I'd be glad to!"

"Thanks, Pavel," she said, with such genuine feeling that Pavel's heart began pounding. He couldn't remember the last time she'd spoken to him like that. "Thanks, but... I don't know. Mama needs support. She's got no one else, and I'm over here..."

After their conversation, which was ultimately inconclusive, he sat for a long time in the warm, electric night. He drummed his fingers on the strangely half-empty screen of his alarm clock. The room rang with silence and the mosquito buzz of the desk lamp, and still he sat there, just sitting, sitting. What if she did come back? Six months, even three months ago he would have given everything. But now? The circumstances were understandable. But paradoxically there was an undercurrent of resentment and disappointment. Resentment because she would be abandoning her dream, which had already cost both of them so much. Disappointment because he was already prepared to confront the situation. To struggle. To fight back. He was ready to go against the grain, to smash up his entire life for the sake of his goal. But now? What if she did decide to come back?

She hadn't decided anything yet.

There weren't many cars outside at all now. A taxi crept past in a predatory fashion just as he finally turned the light off: time to sleep.

The following morning he wrestled obstinately with the rickety shelves in the kitchen. He managed to find some old coffee. It had gone hard, like a mineral. Just then he noticed an old tin can, a product of one of the Comecon countries; he wasn't in the mood to try and decipher the battered Latin letters right now (it might have been Polish, or perhaps Hungarian), and when he was younger the idea had never entered his head. Back then he had been fascinated by this can, by its cobalt blue colour, which even now retained some of its former brilliance. Again, he was reminded of Maxim. One vivid memory in particular stood out. Aged twelve or thirteen, Pavel was following his second cousin round like a puppy, his mouth hanging open with admiration. They were temporarily sharing a bedroom, and one evening, when the same desk lamp was quietly burning and the room was drowned in shadows, Maxim reverentially brought this tin can in from the kitchen. Bending the peak of his baseball cap, he stuck it into the can.

"What's that for?" asked little Pavel, holding his breath.

"If you want to be one of the gang, you have to bend the peak a bit, without breaking it. The best way is to fold it a bit like that and then leave it in a can overnight."

"Have you got a can like that out in the sticks, then?" Totally awestruck, Pavel was prepared to believe even this.

Maxim frowned at the expression "out in the sticks".

"No, I used a glass jar. But that works better, actually."

He was so ostentatiously offhand about it! Pavel envied it all desperately – the glass jar, the gang, the tattered fake Adidas baseball cap, such as he could never even hope to own.

So pathetic. Such cheap, provincial showing off! Even a child wouldn't have fallen for it. Settling into the front passenger seat of the Audi, which held his sides like laughter, Pavel gave a scornful smile.

It was probably a good thing that he'd known Maxim since childhood, although he was embarrassed by the memories. He knew where he'd come from, how far he'd risen. The true cost of all his contrived and painstakingly nurtured habits, everything Maxim used to impress those who barely knew him. Brutal charm, success, generosity, a kind of health (spiritually speaking)... Pavel had seen it all in embryonic form. Maybe not exactly, but something spiteful and envious – the desire to seize with his teeth, to force his way through, to trample over everything. Sheer bluff. The old money had still been in circulation back then, with the same pictures but a lot more zeroes. Millions instead of hundreds. When Maxim was getting ready to go out for the evening, to conquer the big city, he would arrange his pitiful banknotes carefully into a pile so that the biggest note was always on top.

Armed with these images as though they were his secret

trump cards, Pavel cast a victorious sideways glance at the driver's seat.

The driver's mood was visibly changing, by measure of the extent to which they were stuck in the traffic jam. This time they were holding the meeting in a hall at the Railroad Worker House of Culture, a crimson building with columns on the outskirts of the city, where all the roads ran down to the station. The infrastructure in places like this had been terrible ever since the construction of the Trans-Siberian Railway. The traffic was gridlocked all day. Maxim hadn't thought of this and he was already losing his temper, drumming his fingers on the steering wheel. In theory, they shouldn't have been late for the meeting, but now everything was going wrong, and this Napoleon – oh, he didn't like it when things didn't go according to plan!

"I can't remember whether or not I called Fedosov," came Elya's voice from the back seat. She had picked the wrong moment to express her concerns, and Maxim shouted straight back at her,

"I can't believe you haven't managed to ruin everything for us yet!"

Pavel concealed a smirk. In a strange way he liked being able to see through his enemy, gauging his reactions and occasionally pulling his strings, like a puppet.

When they arrived, Maxim would do some breathing exercises to calm himself down. Then he would start to work the room. By the time it came to the buffet in the foyer of the House of Culture he would already be charm personified, and the elderly ladies would eagerly raise their freckled hands like swans to be kissed by him.

Well, the elderly ladies were in for a surprise tonight, as were their fellow guests. Tonight Pavel and his cohorts were planning to mount their first public attack on ARTavia (which explained why Pavel was so calm, before the storm). It was time to stop these "kings of the world", who thought that they could get away with anything.

"Where do you think you're going?" Maxim yelled at another driver who was hermetically sealed inside his own car, even though he himself had mounted the pavement in order to escape the traffic jam. He turned round, twisting his whole body backwards and furiously turning the steering wheel. Cheerful again, he winked at them.

"Sorted. Let's get out of here," he said, and they lurched off through the labyrinths of outbuildings in the residential district, which remembered the round-the-clock thunder of trains rolling to war.

Maxim had other characteristics, of course, ones that in different circumstances Pavel might have agreed to consider positive. For example, he never let anything get him down and tenaciously sought a way out of even the most hopeless situations. He was forever coming up with creative solutions, and he never seemed to run out of ideas. Even when he wasn't working. For example, today at the office he had picked up a glossy magazine from Elya's desk. His attention had been caught by a completely unremarkable advert for age-defying moisturizers on the back cover.

"Look at that slogan, it's terrible – what a waste! They could have made it so much better. If it had been up to me... Imagine a gaudy bedroom and a dressing table in the background, with a mirror. There's a woman sitting in front of it with her back to us and a man standing in the foreground, in profile. He's got a bald patch and he's wearing a suit. The idea is that the woman's putting her make-up on, and her husband has walked past and stopped. Right, so the man looks like Putin, which is easy enough to imitate, and the woman – like his wife Ludmila. Again, not a problem."

"Very bold," said Pavel, taking a mug out of the cupboard.

"I know. So, 'Putin' has spotted this magazine that features an advert for moisturizing cream, and he's standing there holding it so that you can see the slogan: 'Block 97% of free radicals'. And there's an asterisk by the 97%, which always adds a bit of intrigue. Now that would be a good advert! What do you think?"

"Very clever. You know, you remind me of a friend of mine. He's always coming up with stuff like that too. It just seems to spill out of him. Honestly, it's unbelievable."

"Is he in advertising?" asked Maxim, intrigued.

"No, he's a writer. Sort of."

Pavel was surprised to realize, for the first time, that Maxim and Igor genuinely did have something in common: the stories they came up with. Both were perpetually creating adventures for themselves, inventing things and living in their imaginary surroundings, unwilling to see or hear anything that could shatter these fictional worlds. On the contrary, they were prepared to eliminate anyone who got in the way of their fantasies. One of them, whose stories were invented for his mediocre prose, lived his life – happily and harmlessly – under the illusion that he was a talented writer. The other thought he was James Bond, feverishly jumping from the wing of a plane onto the roof of a car, irresistibly invincible. Today he happened to be involved in the ARTavia scam. Tomorrow would be another chapter in his thrilling adventure novel. And as the main character, he thought the novel would never end.

Finally, they arrived. The gaudy foyer of the Railroad Worker was a confectioner's mad vision in granite, with daylight lamp tubes fastened to the delicate ceiling like specks of sanity. The lamps dated back to Soviet times: some almost light-blue, some pinkish. Unfortunately it was not the most flattering light for red-wine-stained lips. So Pavel uncorked a bottle of white first, with professional expertise: once his career in the aviation industry was over he could always get a job as a bartender. Ha! The pre-conference buffet was just beginning. The assembled guests – just a few at first, then more and more – were happy and sociable this evening, probably because it had been such a sunny day.

Maxim greeted them all individually, bowing courteously, asking them how they were, sometimes asking after their families, remembering who owned which business, shaking hands with the city's elite... No, this one would be all right, come what may.

"Is it true that you're planning to start flying to St Petersburg?" asked a black-haired lady in glasses, haughty and aloof as a crow. The director of a modelling agency.

"Not yet, unfortunately, but it's under consideration," Maxim replied with a practised smile.

"Such a pity! I have to go there next month, and I really don't want to fly with anyone else. I just don't want to take the risk."

Just then Olga walked in. She was so beautiful that Pavel, who had paused with a bottle in his hand, didn't even recognize her at first. She looked like a film star. She wore her hair up, and her make-up accentuated her eyes, which were usually grey but now looked almost turquoise. She was wearing a long, light blue evening dress. Everyone was looking at her.

Olga moved around the room as all eyes were riveted on her. She caught sight of Pavel. Her eyes were radiant.

"Olga Evgenievna, good evening!" Maxim moved swiftly over to her, bowed and kissed her hand. "Thank you for gracing us with your beauty. Would you like a glass of wine?"

"Thank you."

Pavel approached with three glasses of golden Muscat. They all took a sip.

"Please give my best regards to Mr Lvov," purred Maxim. "How is business?"

"Everything's fine, thank you for asking."

"When are you going to use your gold membership card, Olga Evgenievna? When will we have the pleasure of seeing you on board an ARTavia flight?"

The polite small talk lasted for about four minutes, until Maxim spotted the regional health minister and began to take his leave.

"I'm afraid I must excuse myself."

"Not for long, I hope," said Olga, proffering her hand flirtatiously, imperiously. "I'll miss your company!"

They smiled at each other.

"How are you feeling, Olga Evgenievna?" asked Pavel, imitating his boss's intonation.

"Simply marvellous!"

They drank their wine with laughter in their eyes. Then they strolled casually into a corner of the foyer. They stood there for a little while, to make sure they weren't being watched, then Olga handed Pavel her glass and slipped through the carved doors. Pavel smiled at the other guests and went to open the red wine.

They would be going through into the hall in about ten minutes: plenty of time for Olga to do what she had to do. Her elegant clutch bag was stuffed with pieces of paper folded in four. She was going to put one on every seat. No one had seen her leave the foyer, the way ahead was clear, and it would be impossible to find out who had gone into the hall before everyone else.

There wasn't much text on the leaflets, but they'd used a

variety of fonts to make them easier to read. Igor had spent the whole of the previous day printing them out. All the facts that they'd managed to find out about ARTavia had been included.

What next? As the leaflets had been placed on the individual seats, every client who had come to the meeting would pick one up and open it. Maxim certainly wasn't going to run along the rows gathering them up. Although Pavel would have liked to see him try.

There was a little wine left in Olga's glass. Before drinking it, Pavel clinked the glass against the enormous Imperial mirror.

"To our victory!"

CHAPTER 13

The street lamp peered into the stairwell through the dusty windows, focussing its attentions on the second floor, which resembled the inside of a chemical retort. The air rising up from below smelled of the basement, metal pipes, homelessness and old age. The thick, glassy reflections that fell across their faces made them look inanimate, like images from old, faded photos. Igor and Pavel were sitting on newspapers that they'd spread out on the stairs, after taking them out of the postboxes downstairs. The composition required a bottle of port, but they didn't have any.

They sat there in silence. Waiting.

"Jesus, how much longer?" exploded Pavel. "We've been sitting here for forty minutes! Call him and find out where the hell he's got to!"

"Chill out, Pavel. Remember, nerve cells don't replenish themselves like reproductive cells do!"

If only Danil had left them the key to his grandmother's apartment... Then they wouldn't be stuck out here on the stairs, like the olden days. Like the pre-mobile era, when they would spend hours waiting around in the agreed places, holding forlorn bouquets, turning up late, losing one another in the chaos of the city. These days, everyone was connected. Such miscommunications no longer occurred... Well, they did, but only when certain individuals were lacking in brains.

They had been in touch with Danil throughout the day, arranging what time to meet and other details, because it was important to get everything right. Unfortunately, there was something else important that Danil had to do beforehand. Yet another meeting with his role-playing cronies, of course. This prior engagement was set in stone, but Danil had assured them that he'd be free by 8 p.m... 9 p.m...

By 9.30 p.m. he was obviously just making up excuses.

Now it was 10 p.m. and they were still there, sitting in front of a locked door, mildly enraged: was that bastard ever going to show up? True, they could have done it without him. But as luck would have it the flyers, along with everything else they needed, were locked in the apartment.

By rights, Igor should probably have been the one getting most upset, but he was somehow managing to retain his sense of humour. He took the leaden newspaper out from under him.

"Oh look, the horoscope. Aries, here we go, this is yours. 'Today is a good day for new beginnings and business projects, whereas travel is best avoided.' What do you reckon, does our mission count as a business project?"

"It says 'day', not night."

"True. Right, Sagittarius..."

Pavel wasn't listening. His legs were aching uncomfortably from sitting in the same position for too long, and also from the draughty stairwell. Outside it was growing warmer day by day; the thaw had begun, and drips were hammering onto the metal roofs. But not now. In the evening everything froze again and the light from the street lamp pierced the pale, icy prisms.

"Can't you call him again?"

"What are you getting so worked up about, Pasha?" asked Igor, putting the newspaper to one side. "He might be another hour, but so what? We won't be going out till later anyway. We're all right sitting here, aren't we? Or are you getting cold? Hey, maybe we could go and get something to warm us up, what do you think?" Igor winked.

"I don't like the idea of Olga turning up and seeing us sitting here like tramps. Are you going to offer her a bit of newspaper to sit on as well?"

"Look, what exactly is the problem?"

Either Igor was stupid and genuinely didn't get it, or he was winding him up, but either way Pavel wasn't going to let him get away with it.

"What do you mean, what's the problem?" he began. "Just think about it! What are we, street yobs who hang out in stairwells? Are we going to ask her to sit with us on the stairs? Maybe we should go and get something to warm us up, as you suggest... What the hell will she think of us? She's such a..."

"Lady," Igor prompted cheerfully.

"Stop taking the piss, will you? You didn't see her that night... At the House of Culture. She was... magical. I don't even know how to put it. I was completely blown away."

A silence hung between them, which on Pavel's part was clearly wistful; Igor broke it with a short, dry laugh.

"Well, well! It's a clear-cut diagnosis. First comes love, then comes marriage..."

Pavel leapt to his feet, ready to punch Igor.

"You don't know what you're talking about!" he

exclaimed, almost shouting. He was so upset he felt like crying. Igor had to play a conciliatory tune to try and calm him down, by reminding him that they were friends.

They heard the sound of footsteps below. When Danil appeared on the second floor landing, they didn't recognize him straight away: the light from the icy street lamp was falling on him from behind, illuminating the fine hairs that long-haired people always have sticking up from their heads if they don't comb their hair before it dries. Danil had obviously either been to a *banya* or got his hair wet some other way. He'd clearly had a good evening.

When Danil caught sight of his friends and started waving like a maniac, no further doubt remained.

"Igor, he's wasted!"

"Shh."

They all went up into the apartment. Igor insisted that their host take a cold shower. Once the lights were on in all the rooms, burning in different shades of weak yellow, the overall effect was quite cosy and seemed to warm them up. They put the kettle on, all the same, and the gas flame began to lick its base with passion.

They had already done the preparations for this evening, and everything lay in perfect order on the old table, which bore the angular scorch mark of an iron: thick masking tape that reeked of Chinese chemicals, two cheap Stanley knives and a neat pile of flyers. Pavel picked up the pile, which wasn't particularly large. "Dear citizens... Con artists are operating in our city... The circumstances necessitate a public appeal..." Then a few facts. The many hours Pavel himself had spent in the con artists' den had not been in vain.

At first Pavel had been sceptical about Igor's idea of sticking flyers up in the street, like underground rebels.

Would it work? Would anyone bother to read them? People aren't generally interested in helping others. Once, at the beginning of autumn, when the sky was lemon yellow and tinged with smoke, Pavel had been walking across the small square near the city entertainment complex before some show or other. By way of a warm-up, four young men were beating up another man who had obviously been drinking. Another group of lads walked past. The victim appealed to them for help. One of the lads walked over and callously "helped"... by kicking his blood-covered face. Then they went on their way, laughing their heads off.

But Pavel hadn't helped the unfortunate individual either, who was probably guilty of nothing more than making a stupid, drunken joke about the fact that their pierced ears made them look "like girls".

What could he have done to help?

What could any member of the public do to help fight ARTavia?

Of course, the best approach was to appeal directly to the target audience – all those deluded chief accountants and businessmen, who met once a week for their brainwashing fix. They had been so confused by the leaflets. But in all honesty, Pavel hadn't expected anything to come of their campaign. They were dealing with people traumatized by the fear of flying, after all. Was it even possible to get through to them? It's a very specific mind set.

Pavel had noticed something interesting about these people. He had a little theory that he hadn't fully explored. (He was in the kitchen, where the steam was belching from the kettle, and he wanted to tip the dregs from the teapot into the toilet but the bathroom was locked; Danil was wallowing drunkenly and leisurely in the bath.) Whenever these "ladies and gentlemen" got together and began talking quietly amongst themselves, whether it was in the gaudy hall of a House of Culture or in the departure lounge before a flight, a strange kind of adrenalin would spread through the air. A peculiar kind of excitement. It seemed very familiar, though it took Pavel a while to work out what it was. When he was younger he had read several books of a certain type, one after the other. He had found them on his parents' bookshelves, which was hardly surprising as they had been fans of The Beatles and the poet Andrei Voznesensky in their youth. They had been the kind of people to get off at the end of a suburban line with a tent and a guitar; as the commuter train receded into the distance the idle engine on its tail would look back at them until it disappeared, like a tadpole with eyebrows. These books literally brimmed with a combination of delirious enthusiasm for technology, the sky and friendship, questionable literary merit and a certain exhilarating risk. Books such as Golovanov's *Thunder's Blacksmiths* and Granin's *Into the Storm*. He'd also come across a story in a tattered old copy of *Ural* magazine, called "People and Planes in the Night". They were all about what it was like to fly in the 1960s. About skipping up the staircase of progress into the intoxicating unknown. About the feeling of euphoria that preceded the possibility of death.

Surprising as it might seem, something similar was occurring right now. Pavel could sense it. Maybe flying had gone from being the cheap, mundane (and basically boring) business it had been for at least the past twenty years to having an element of risk about it once again. Thanks to the press. Thanks to the general mood of hysteria. The cheerful adrenalin of the 1960s had returned, albeit with a different focal point; then it had been the beauty of progress, but now... Furthermore, there was an added thrill in the knowledge that the technology had remained unchanged. Take the Tu-154, for example. Considering the high-risk ordeals it has been through (the 1979 film *Air Crew* springs to mind), you can't help the lurching feeling in the pit of your stomach when you board one today.

Maybe someone would write a new *Thunder's Blacksmiths*? Maybe it'll be Igor, thought Pavel, and this made him laugh.

Olga turned up about ten minutes later. A little out of breath because she'd been hurrying, her cheeks attractively flushed. She was wearing a light and elegant fitted fur jacket, which gleamed in the light, and an unusual flat, round fur hat. She was so petite, so perfectly formed, that Pavel immediately stepped back into the hallway to make way for her.

"Sorry, I got held up. I said I was staying at a friend's for the night... Well, the daughter of my parents' friends. Thankfully she lives in the city, not with her parents. So I had to call in and see her on the way here."

While Igor busied himself making tea, politely keeping his distance, Pavel and Olga made themselves comfortable in the living room. Pavel was amused by the way she took her fur coat off and arranged it carefully on a hanger, then adjusted her top in front of the mirror. She had obviously planned her outfit carefully, knowing that she would be spending the night outside and the warmth of the day was deceptive. Whereas Pavel hadn't given it the slightest thought, fool that he was. For some reason this amused him so much that he started laughing. Olga laughed too.

"Hey, I thought of something today. Have you read *Into the Storm*, or *Thunder's Blacksmiths*?"

"No. Are they any good?"

"I'll let you borrow them, if I can find them at home. Basically..."

Basically what, she never found out. Danil emerged

from the bathroom and shuffled wetly down the hallway, with nothing to protect his modesty. Everything swung freely from side to side, like a living creature that had rolled in grey dust. The look on his face was completely unperturbed, the kind you sometimes see on bass players when they're on stage and oblivious to the fact that the column of ash from their cigarette has just collapsed onto them.

Olga's eyes almost fell out of their sockets.

"What the fuck are you doing?" exclaimed Pavel. "We've got guests!"

Danil focussed, gave a yelp, turned around and fled.

"I never realized that long-haired boys looked like girls from behind," remarked Olga, and Pavel was surprised at how quickly she had regained her composure.

"Olga, please, I'm sorry, he..."

"Don't worry about it!" she said, laughing. "There's never a dull moment with you guys!"

Guys, indeed. That wasn't from her usual vocabulary.

Igor stuck his head out of the kitchen. "Maybe we should go without him? The state he's in..."

But just then a voice came from the bathroom. "Hey, you're not leaving me out! I'm ready! I just need someone to bring me my trousers..."

That night a Dalavia Tu-214 aircraft, en route from Moscow to Khabarovsk, was forced to return to Domodedovo airport and make an emergency landing. A drop in oil pressure was observed in the right-hand engine ten minutes after take-off, and the captain made the decision to switch the engine off. According to an Interfax report, not one of the 146 passengers on board was injured. At the same time the Russian International News Agency, also quoting the airport press office, reported 142 passengers on board.

Meanwhile our four spent half the night roaming about

the city centre, which was painted obliquely in bright orange and moonlight. Slightly more sober now – or maybe not, it was hard to tell – Danil delighted in the way the thin March ice cracked and shattered. Igor started biting off strips of clear tape (because using scissors when your hands are freezing is more trouble than it's worth), and it took a long time to get rid of the taste in his mouth. Flyers proclaiming the terrible truth about ARTavia were left to flap in the wind, taped at the waist to ornate Soviet lampposts and the notice boards outside the Philharmonic concert hall, which advertised the current program in excruciatingly widely spaced letters. They didn't encounter many others out at that time of night.

It all started to go horribly wrong when they reached the cinema, with its Stalinist rococo facade and heavy decorative urns, cavernous with cigarette ash. Igor was the one who suggested sticking a couple of flyers there. The tape squealed. They stepped back, admiring their handiwork: nice and straight.

"Guys, shhh," Pavel hissed through his teeth. "Don't look round."

A police car, with only its side-lights on, came rolling down one of the back streets. Ve-ery slowly. Its occupants peered at them. A screech of brakes. (They always seem to screech on four-wheel drives.)

"Shit... Shit... Get rid of it, quickly!" Igor panicked. Danil was holding the carrier bag full of flyers, but he didn't react. He just stood there swaying, twitching his nostrils suspiciously.

"Hey, you lot!" barked one of the police officers, as he got out of the car. "Show me some ID!"

It was too late to hide, so they stood there waiting helplessly as the officer walked firmly and authoritatively towards them. A polyurethane truncheon swung beneath his fur jacket, like a symbol of his masculine superiority.

"Didn't you hear me? Your IDs, I said! What are you doing hanging about here at this time of night? Are you drunk? No? Why's he swaying like that, then? We could see him from the car! What have you been drinking? What's in the bag? Come on, let's have a look..."

Igor looked helplessly at the others, grabbed the carrier bag from Danil and held it out.

The police officer, who had a ruddy complexion and was wearing his fur hat pushed back, took out a couple of flyers and stood so that the light fell on them. He whistled to himself.

"Well, I say! Have a look at this, Lyosh. It's some kind of public appeal... 'Dear citizens... We're being conned...' Holy shit! Right, come on then, down to the station. We can sort it out there."

Despair. Desperation.

"Maybe we can come to some agreement..." muttered Igor, but just then Danil, who had remained silent up to this point, merely flaring his nostrils like a stallion, decided to join in.

"Why should we talk to these freaks?" he objected. "Take that!"

Before any of them knew what was happening he had drawn his fist back, like some kind of action hero, and punched the officer's ruddy face so hard that his hat flew off and Danil himself fell over, landing on his backside.

After that it all kicked off. Foreheads collided. Pavel gripped Olga's hand so tightly that it hurt. They ended up in a nearby courtyard without even realizing how they'd got there, and they carried on running, clumsily, slipping about on the ice. No one was running after them. Grunting and swearing, the police officers were busy laying into Danil. Then they lifted him up, holding his hands behind his back, and...

Darkness. The fugitives tried in vain to catch their breath in an out-of-the-way courtyard. They spat thickly in the snow. Panic.

"I can't believe he hit a cop!"

"What an idiot!"

"With his past, too! He'll definitely get sent down now!"

The collective hysteria continued for about five minutes. Igor kicked a snowman. All this time Olga was quiet. Suddenly she said, "Right, I'm going to call Papa. I'll ask him to get Danil out of there. What's his surname?"

"Are you sure you can do that?"

"I don't know. But we have to try. We have to help him."

Clutching her mobile phone and muttering to herself, Olga went off to the other end of the courtyard, where it was completely dark and something was dripping. She was gone for a long time. When she finally came back, she had obviously been crying. Pavel's heart lurched.

"Papa won't help," she said, trying to stop her voice shaking.

"What happened?"

She was unable to hold back any longer and burst into noisy tears.

"He... he shouted at me... Hung up on me... Said that I was lying to him... That I'm roaming the streets, getting into all kinds of trouble... How can I go home now?"

Pavel put his arms around her, stroked her back and tried to calm her down.

It was a disaster.

Ice sculptures had frozen under the drainpipes, and the night was bright with frost.

CHAPTER 14

Dear Pavel,

I tried calling but couldn't get hold of you. It's 4 a.m. your time, and you haven't been online all night. Never mind. You're working full time now, and I can't expect you to spend all night sitting at the computer. I'm proud of you! Seriously.

I wanted to tell you over the phone but I couldn't get through, so now I'm emailing... I just want you to know as soon as possible. I called the doctor (thanks for the number, by the way). Thankfully it's not as serious as they thought when they first examined her, but it's still pretty serious. Mama has to stay in hospital, and she might have to stop work for a while.

I've decided to come home. You'll be able to meet me at the airport at the beginning of April. Actually, if you're feeling particularly heroic you could even meet me in Moscow. Just don't try and talk me out of it. It's too late, anyway, I'm already filling in the withdrawal forms. It's not just about Mama, as I'm sure you're aware. I overestimated my abilities, and it didn't work out for me here. I'm feeling terrible about the way I treated Mama and the way I treated you. It's not right to just abandon people like that. That's why it could never work. It's just a pity it's taken me this long to realize it.

The past four months have been awful. Thank you for waiting for me. Now we can be together. Love N x
P.S. It's 6.20 pm in Pittsburg. 51° F.

In the dense, shivering darkness, the computer screen assaulted his eyes. It was too bright, too intense. Every single overwhelmingly precise letter had become imprinted on his brain. Pavel rubbed his eyes, which felt small and red like a rabbit's. It was already gone 7 a.m. He had decided not to switch the light on in the office and was vaguely aware of the traffic flowing sluggishly beneath the window.

He hadn't bothered going home. He had spent the rest of the night wandering the city, crunching frost underfoot, trying to understand why things had turned out the way they had. They'd been playing a dangerous game, and all he knew was that they'd taken it too far.

He still had no idea what had happened to Danil as his mobile phone kept ringing out, cutting him off politely in two languages. He had put the tearful Olga in a taxi. She had given the driver her address in Red Springs, and her subsequent fate was unknown. And it's all his fault, Pavel thought with icy clarity, as he recognized Maxim's voice in the corridor and now his silhouette on the ribbed glass of the door. He watched as his boss fiddled with the lock for a few moments, then entered the office and switched on the light.

Maxim was so startled he almost cried out.

"What are you doing here so early? And in the dark!"

He slapped the papers down, with *Soviet Sport* on top, and let his car keys clatter to the desk. Maxim never deviated from this ostentatious little routine, whatever mood he was in. Not that you could ever tell what mood he was in.

It was a pervasive northern dawn, that moment when the instigator of festivities lingers behind slightly flushed clouds and everything swells with grey. When the street lamps are still on; white and moon-bright all night, now they seem to be sleeping, lulled into a trance. Multistorey columns of kitchen windows are ablaze. People are waking to the tenacious din of alarm clocks, lying in bed and listening to the lift rising and falling. Khrushchev-era apartments don't have lifts. People laboriously tramp down the stairs instead.

Good mornings happen later. Not now.

He tried calling Danil one more time. No answer. He tried composing a response to Natasha's mail, but his brain wasn't working. All he managed to produce was inane, obliging drivel: no problem, of course he'd meet her in Moscow, no problem, though maybe she didn't need to come back after all... No problem.

"One of our competitors has obviously got it in for us," said Maxim, suddenly. "But which one? I can't work it out. There are five other airlines flying the same route as us, but it's not the sort of thing any of them would do. It just seems a bit childish."

Burdened with his own thoughts, Pavel hadn't even noticed that his boss had been on the phone all morning.

"What's happened?"

"Apparently some gang went round last night putting flyers up. Probably the same rubbish as those leaflets at the Railroad Worker. I need to find out the details. It's all a bit vague at the moment."

It was strange, but Pavel didn't really feel anything. He didn't need to hide his reaction, like a character in a spy film; he was genuinely surprised by his own internal wilderness.

"Flyers?" he repeated, for no reason other than that it seemed to be the appropriate response.

"Yes. It's no big deal, we'll get to the bottom of it – who, where, and so on. Otherwise this nonsense will just carry on. Who's behind it?"

Pavel made a noise like an echo. He touched his keyboard. He looked out of the window, where an egg yolk sun had spilled into the sky and was spreading over the windows of buildings and everywhere at once. Igor called at 10.30 a.m. He got straight to the point: Danil had suffered a further beating at the police station. He had got home that morning and was sleeping at the moment. Igor didn't know how badly he'd been injured; he hadn't seen him in person, they'd just spoken by phone. Briefly, no doubt, considering that Danil would have been nursing the remnants of a hangover and a bloody lip. It was entirely possible that he'd come home to an empty apartment, collapsed onto his bed, developed a fever and died from a brain haemorrhage in his sleep an hour later. Pavel was already imagining this scenario as he sat there paralyzed, staring at a fixed point in space, clutching and releasing his mobile phone. It was roughly the same as what he saw when he tried to imagine the nightmare that had occurred in Cheboksary the previous century.

"Ha ha ha!" Maxim burst out laughing.

Pavel slowly turned to look at him.

"This article's hilarious! It's about the President congratulating Tereshkova on her seventieth birthday," said Maxim, shaking his copy of *Kommersant*. "Listen to this... 'Standing in the reception hall of the President's official residence in Novo-Ogarevo, Valentina Tereshkova spoke so loudly and with such excitement that the senior government officials in the room across the hallway must surely have heard her passionate cry "To Mars! To Mars!" Nevertheless, she concedes that a number of factors need to be considered before submitting a detailed project proposal to the President. "We must identify a landing site, for a start," Ms Tereshkova mused, deeply concerned. "And a launch site for the flight from Mars to the waiting space station. On a more general note, we should be studying planets outside the terrestrial group too. We should all be concerned at the number and variety of visitors we receive from outer space." She must have seen the look on my face, because she hastily added, "Comets, I mean, and asteroids.""""

Maxim couldn't read any further. He was almost falling off his chair with laughter, throwing his head back so far that Pavel caught an involuntary glimpse of his back teeth. A perfect row. And the rest of Maxim was just as healthy. He was cheerful, well groomed and very pleased with himself. He liked nice cars. He liked to enjoy life which sometimes meant taking pleasure in laughing at the imperfection all around him. Pavel dropped his mobile phone onto his desk and narrowed his eyes. Maxim took this as an invitation to continue and picked up the newspaper again.

""""Is it true that you're prepared to stay there, to contemplate not coming back to Earth?" I asked. "Why would I want to come back?" she replied, looking into my eyes. "What's the point?""""

Pavel waited until Maxim had finished laughing.

"Do you really find that funny? Someone as young and rich, as..." Pavel paused "...successful as you, mocking an elderly woman?"

The phrase "defending an old lady's honour" sprang to mind. Where was that from?

Maxim stared at him in astonishment. The smile slipped from his face. Pavel continued, ve-ery slowly.

"It's not even the fact that Tereshkova's getting on a bit, or that she's a woman and it's ungentlemanly. It's the fact that she has a dream, and she was brave enough to share it with the world. She's had the same goal all her life. Is that really a reason to make a laughing stock out of her? I don't know. For people like you, it probably is. Personally, I envy those who have a goal in life. But I guess that's my problem."

He was reminded of Natasha, of endless autumn evenings when the mist settled in your lungs and the street lamps painted the islands of wet leaves around them no colour at all. September. Pavel paced round the puddles in the dark courtyards, because Natasha spent every evening studying English: all night, every night, without complaining. Just tearfully gulping caffeine.

The back of his neck ached with hatred. He had to breathe out before continuing. "As for you... you've got no principles, none at all. I wish we weren't related. Not only have you got no sense of decency... You've got no brain, no thoughts of your own. Nothing ever bothers you, does it? You're so bloody smug."

An unpleasant silence hung in the air. Maxim paused before launching into his response.

"You... you... Who the hell do you think you are?"

The tirade continued. Pavel caught the word "nobody", but he had already slammed the door behind him with such satisfaction that the glass panel cracked. He shouted back that he quit. Now he was free to go wherever he liked.

Spring. Boots that were loose and smelled sour. Damp snow dripping rustily from American maples. Pavel kicked the snow. He thought about going to the park near Natasha's house, where parents and buggies had been replaced by the agonizing scrape of sledge runners across the concrete paths. He thought about buying a bottle of beer, breathtakingly cold, and drinking it by the sad skeleton of the climbing frame, but...

But an hour later he was sitting beneath the yellow lampshades waiting for a cappuccino, and from the furious spluttering that was coming from the kitchen it sounded as though all the staff were getting covered in it.

He didn't know what he was doing there, why Olga had invited him. Neither did she. She looked down into her cup with a kind of childish stubbornness, pursing her lips.

Everything about her seemed faded and drawn. She wasn't trying to look attractive today.

"How are things at home? What did your father say?" asked Pavel. This was the only thing he could think of to talk about. She just waved his questions away.

He didn't feel remotely like shouldering the burden of all this guilt: Danil getting beaten up, Olga getting kicked out.

"Danil got beaten up."

He told her briefly what had happened, adding that he and Igor had agreed to go round to Danil's place that evening, to find out what was going on.

"Just the two of you? But what about me?"

Suddenly alert, Pavel looked in astonishment at her wobbling chin and her eyes too, which seemed to be filling with tears. It hadn't even occurred to him to invite her. What was the point now? It was hardly a social occasion.

"I don't know if that's such a good idea... We're going to see how he is, what kind of state he's in. We need to make him go and see a doctor. At least get him some medicine."

"So? I can come with you. There's nothing to be embarrassed about, I've already seen him naked – or have you forgotten?"

Olga was smiling now, having reduced everything to a joke. She'd pulled herself together. But after a pause, she added almost piteously, "We're a team, aren't we?"

Ah, so that was it. Pavel understood. She saw herself as an upper class terrorist. In her naive, cinematic view of the world there was no way back, she had rejected her home and family, they were all that remained. For some reason he was infuriated by this naivety, this childishness.

Danil opened the door himself, proud that he'd managed to forestall Igor's fussing, and tried his best to prove to them that everything was fine. This over-the-top optimism was a mask for his fear, which was still visible if you looked deep into his eyes, ignoring the bruising and the swelling. But this was categorically impossible.

"I'm fine! There's no need to make such a fuss," he assured them, though he admitted later that it hurt to walk and he kept needing to pee. He chose not to mention the blood in his stool.

Of all of them, Igor was the most depressed. He was silent and subdued. He slammed a bottle of vodka down on the table, but when Danil held out a shot glass he barked, "Don't even think about it! There's no way you're drinking vodka, the state your kidneys are in! Are you going to go and see the doctor?"

They downed a shot, then another. They hadn't prepared any food to chase the vodka with, but Igor had brought some juice and Danil fetched some of his grandmother's pickles from the larder. At first they thought they'd gone off: the enormous cucumbers, which looked like sunken submarines, were coated with a thick deposit.

"They're fine, it's only mustard. My grandmother's secret recipe. Just wash it off under the tap."

Narrowing his eyes almost spitefully, Pavel watched as Olga fastidiously swallowed her shot, then humbly bit into a pickled submarine. He wondered whether she'd ever drunk vodka like this before.

None of them spoke. The only sound was the rumbling echo of armchairs from the newly renovated apartment next door.

Pavel savagely crunched into a pickle. "My boss knows about the flyers," he said, to break the silence. "Someone called him. I don't know how much he knows, but he said he was going to get to the bottom of it."

"Shit," groaned Igor. "Now they're going to be looking

for us. And they'll probably find us, too. This is bad... very bad... Did you say anything to them? What did they ask you about the flyers?"

The latter questions were addressed to Danil, who guiltily shook his head. He couldn't remember.

When they tired of sitting round the table (which didn't take long), Olga tipsily suggested that they might benefit from a bit of culture. In the absence of any art house films they decided to watch Spielberg's *War of the Worlds*, starring Tom Cruise. They took the rest of the vodka into the living room and sat around the computer. Olga put her arms around Pavel, pressing her cheek to the back of his neck.

On screen the Martians, armed with devices called tripods, were destroying and burning everything in their path, while the Earthlings ran about in aimless herds; Danil was nodding off, whereas Olga was getting more and more excited. She was kissing, licking and even nibbling Pavel's ear. On a purely physical level it was not unpleasant, of course. But it felt strange.

One of the characters was trying to explain to another that since these tripods had been on Earth prior to the invasion, there must have been traitors in their midst. He could remember some film critics alluding to a similarity with the weapons used in the Beslan massacre. But it reminded Pavel of something more innocent. When he was younger, he had been fascinated by a certain old car: there was something almost alien about it, and it was always covered in grey dust, as though it had recently been unearthed. It was the vehicle used by an unshaven local farmer to deliver potatoes to their primary school canteen, and it was completely different from all the Volga and Pobeda cars that he knew. The way it was crammed full of potatoes made it look more like a lorry – dirty and worn-out by the village roads. All the children would run out to look at it. The images Pavel subsequently saw showed only shiny, new versions of the same car, so it took a while for him to realize that the object of his childhood fascination had in fact been a 1950s ZIM limousine.

Meanwhile Olga was becoming more and more insistent.

"Come with me," she whispered into his cold, wet ear. Then she got up and walked to the bathroom, without waiting to see if he would follow.

In the bathroom her confidence began to desert her. As she was unbuttoning her tight-fitting white blouse, she suddenly stopped. When Pavel took her hand he could feel her trembling.

"Take your clothes off!" he demanded, not recognizing his own voice. A joyous rage and a kind of daring were growing alongside his arousal. The incongruity of the setting just added an extra thrill: this clean, pink, nervous girl in the filth of a bachelor's bathroom, with socks and pants hanging everywhere, stray hairs of every variety, even pictures of naked women that Danil had stuck to the tiles. And she didn't hesitate to rest the most intimate part of her body on the edge of the dirty bath.

"Take your clothes off too," she said gently. Pavel ignored her. Just as he dismissed the idea of using a condom (although he could have asked Danil for anything). He wanted to take her roughly, forcefully. He wanted to be the way he never could with Natasha.

But first, a good look at her breasts. He wanted to squeeze them. Knead them. Olga obviously went to an expensive tanning salon, one where they stuck special tape over her nipples. There was no other explanation for the fact that her breasts were lightly tanned, caramel coloured, whereas her nipples were light pink, with visible veins, like the inside of an unripe watermelon. Positive and negative.

She cried out, begging him to stop. He was hurting her. "Louder!" he urged.

He had to think about all kinds of things in order to stop himself coming too quickly when he was with Natasha, but that didn't worry him now. He knew it would take about three minutes. He knew that Olga, almost in tears, was a long way from pleasure. But he didn't care. This was all about what he wanted.

He said nothing, but his breathing grew louder and louder until she realized...

"Not inside, please!"

That was the trigger. He thrust himself into her as far as he could and froze as the first shot was fired. Then another. And another. Then, after a long-drawn-out pause, one final shot.

She perched on the edge of the bath, breathing hard, crucified, crushed, defiled.

Pavel went out into the living room, where the Earthlings were valiantly battling the Martians. His friends turned round.

"Was she a virgin?" asked Igor.

"Have we got any more vodka?" asked Danil.

CHAPTER 15

Early in the morning of Saturday 17 March 2007, the weather at Samara Kurumoch Airport took a turn for the worse. Visibility decreased from 2,300 to 200 metres in just forty minutes. Pilots were warned to expect "patches of dense fog"; journalists were told of pre-existing "adverse weather conditions and an accumulation of negative tendencies". As a UTair Tupolev Tu-134 flying from Surgut to Belgorod was coming in to land for a scheduled stopover in Samara it missed the runway, hit the ground, overturned and broke apart. Six passengers were killed. The remaining forty-four survived, as did all seven members of the crew.

The snow cover at the landing site was measured and found to be 57 cm deep. This cushion may well have been what protected the aircraft from the scraping of metal on concrete, from explosion, from the flames of hell.

It was ultimately decided that pilot error was to blame, though the unusually complicated weather conditions were to be taken into consideration. From their hospital beds (it was reported in the press that the captain was walking about the hospital barefoot, because they couldn't find any slippers to fit him), the crew agreed that the air traffic controllers were to blame. The flight engineer expressed doubts over the condition of the aircraft's instrument landing system. The airline management requested that the incident be considered the "result of extreme stress" and promised that no disciplinary action would be taken.

The passengers spoke willingly to reporters. One of them was less concerned about his torn ear than about his briefcase full of documents, which had been lost somewhere in the remains of economy class. One of the flight attendants spoke rather coquettishly of her surprise at finding herself walking on the snow in her tights. She had no idea what had happened to her shoes.

"The guys from work called me yesterday, trying to cheer me up. 'You'll live to be a hundred,' they said. Because when the fuselage broke apart I thought that's it, I'm going to die, it's going to explode! And I begged God not to tear me to pieces... I couldn't bear the thought of lying there without any legs! But the explosion never happened. So I crawled on my hands and knees... This huge pile of debris, arms and legs sticking out of it, and I'm crawling and shouting automatically, 'Please keep calm!' Some of the passengers joked back, 'We're perfectly calm, everything's fine!'"

An astonishing incident: when the wreckage of the fuselage had settled awkwardly on its side, a door was flung open and the glassy-eyed pilots clambered out of the cockpit and into the cabin. A voice accosted them from the front row, with the kind of mundane remark commonly heard on public transport: "Hey, you ought to look where you're going!"

Vadim from Belgorod: "We searched the whole cabin for a knife to cut the seatbelts, because lots of people were hanging upside down in their seats and couldn't undo them. I hit my head badly, and if it wasn't for my leather jacket I would have hurt my back as well. Incidentally, I knew something was wrong back in Surgut... The plane looked like it was falling apart. I saw rust on one of the wings. And when it crashed, the bit where the wing was reinforced burst into flames. We covered the fire with snow. It took twenty minutes for the rescuers to reach us! So there was heavy fog, I get it, but we were waiting on the runway all that time!"

Evgeny from Tyumen: "It was the most horrible feeling. Our plane had just crashed, and no one was coming to help us!"

All the passengers recalled those long minutes they spent stranded in the fog, near the fragments of the Tupolev aircraft, which must have looked more like the discarded stages of a rocket. Stranded and helpless, they just didn't know what to do. They started switching on their mobile phones. You must have heard it before, the collective Ode to Joy that starts up when a plane has landed and is taxiing to the stand, a cacophony of ringtones and bleeps... Only this time there was no joy. For some reason no one was able to get a signal, but they stubbornly persisted in tormenting their keypads.

The captain: "The rescue vehicles drove straight past us – twice! Can you believe that?"

Some found their own way to the airport building. Some met the fire engines that were heading noisily and blindly towards them. An airport bus was eventually sent to pick up the last remaining passengers, but even then the authorities faced the challenge of rounding up those who had panicked and left Kurumoch altogether.

Another astonishing incident: no announcement had been made inside the airport building. The arrival information board simply stated that the flight had been delayed. An elderly couple were waiting for their nephew from Surgut. He approached them from behind and said hello. Surprised exclamations, embraces.

"But how did you get here?"

The boy waved his hand airily. "Oh, our plane crashed."

The passengers complained that no one seemed to know what to do with them. They didn't know where to take them, where to put them, how to keep them together. How to occupy them. Staff at a local bar recalled some of the passengers from the ill-fated flight coming in and ordering beer and snacks. They were barely capable of exchanging even a few words with the waitresses.

The press reports sounded all too familiar. An editorial article in *Komsomolskaya Pravda* began with the words, "More emergency situations than in a madhouse!" Alexander Shengardt, chief designer of the Tu-154, made the following statement: "Plane crashes will never stop happening, anywhere in the world, because flying is not a natural state for humans – it's simply a necessary measure, a means to an end."

Meanwhile doctors in Samara noted with satisfaction that all of the injured passengers were able to give their names and the phone numbers of their next of kin. A total of twenty-eight passengers were admitted to the 18th Kalinin Regional Clinical Hospital, suffering from head injuries, fractures and open wounds.

Oh, those depressing hospital corridors! With their lumpy linoleum, their indifferent ceilings and the distant crashing of pots and pans...

Lists detailing the patients' surnames, wards and temperature readings had been stuck directly onto the green wall, which had been repainted so many times it was completely uneven. Pavel frowned as he attempted to decipher the doctor's handwriting. He resorted to guessing at surnames by their contours, until his attention was caught by an entry that read "deceased". He hastily moved away from the wall and cast another hopeful glance at the plump female doctor. Her lips were moving as she consulted her charts. She looked like someone's cuddly grandmother.

"Can't you just let me in?"

"I already told you, no! There's a flu epidemic!" snapped the doctor, sounding not remotely like a cuddly grandmother. Then for some reason she suddenly took pity on him. "Why, are you her son?"

For a split second Pavel's thoughts were all over the place and he wondered, should he lie? What relationship was he to Anna Mikhailovna, anyway? Her "future son-in-law"? No, best not to think about that.

"A friend of the family."

The steely edge returned to the doctor's voice. "In that case, definitely not!" she concluded triumphantly.

The Cardiology Centre had been placed utterly and incontrovertibly under quarantine, as was the case every year when the snow turned to slush. Pavel didn't know this. On the morning of 17 March he had turned up at the draughty glass entrance lobby, and now he was loitering about the reception area like a fool, holding a bulging carrier bag that was obviously full of fruit. Why had he come here without mentioning it to Natasha? Did he want Anna Mikhailovna to tell her afterwards and for her to think favourably of him? Was he atoning for his sins? Or did he simply feel sorry for this tired, worn-out old woman?

Eventually he gave up.

"Can someone at least give her this parcel and this note?"

He had travelled right across the city to get there at the start of visiting hours, too. Part of his journey had been on an unusually long tram with heaters inappropriately placed underneath the seats, which were on full blast. The curly-haired female conductor, her fingers beetroot red after the winter, advised everyone not to leave their bags on the floor in case they melted. Pavel watched the residential district slide past the windows in one long, continuous image, like an old-fashioned film, wearing the detached half smile of someone who has all the time in the world. Today was the first day he'd woken up knowing that he didn't have to go to work. He hadn't set his alarm clock, but in fact he got up even earlier than usual: without the untimely electronic intrusion it had actually been a pleasure to start the day. It was the beginning of a new life.

He had decided not to tell his mother that he'd been fired, for the time being at least. What was the point of upsetting people he cared about as he was on his way out for the day? It could wait until later. Everything could wait until later.

"Young man! Is that your telephone ringing? Can't you hear it?" asked the doctor, lowering her glasses.

Of course he could hear it. He'd forgotten to switch the sound off. He frowned in irritation.

Olga had called him several times the previous evening. And during the night. She'd been sending text messages too, which he had deleted without reading. What could he possibly say to her? He dreaded the sound of her voice, dreaded the thought that she might start crying quietly into the phone, convulsively catching her breath, which would make him want to throw himself from the seventh floor window. Or maybe she wouldn't cry... Maybe she was just calling to tell him exactly how much she hated him. It would be easier if he knew what to expect from her. Anything would have been better than this uncertainty. Once or twice during the night, half dreaming, he was convinced that the doorbell was about to ring and Mr Lvov's assistants were going to burst in and attack him, kicking him and leaving him covered in blood, like Danil. He could even have put up with that. Or so it seemed to Pavel as he sat bolt upright in the light from the standard lamp, unable to disentangle his dreams from reality.

"Honestly," sighed the doctor, heaving and swaying like a white sea. "Some people! Wandering about, making so much noise..."

Pavel clutched his treacherous phone and hurried out into the glass lobby, which reverberated with the sound of the doors. When he glanced at the display, he was surprised to see that it wasn't Olga. It was Igor. The thought briefly crossed his mind that she'd resorted to pestering his friends, persuading them to call him on her behalf.

"Hello? Finally! Where are you?"

"At the hospital," sighed Pavel.

"What? Already? How come, did Danil call you?"

The misunderstanding was soon cleared up. It wasn't good news. Igor hastily explained that despite Danil's grumbling, he had done as he was told and gone along to the local hospital that morning. The triage team examined him and were horrified by what they saw. He was urgently admitted to the accident and emergency department. His kidneys and spleen, apparently. The details had been overlooked in Igor's hurry to ask what to bring, who to contact and what to tell them.

"What are we supposed to do now?" asked Igor at the end of their brief conversation. Even more ridiculously, he seemed to be expecting an answer.

"Nothing."

"Maybe we could get together and discuss it this evening?"

"All right then, if you like."

Sadly, the brief charm of the spring morning – charming courtyards, stacks of firewood, the Chaplinesque swaying of trams – had disappeared without trace. Pavel strode furiously away from the Cardiology Centre, almost knocking everyone else from the path. He'd made a real mess of his life – or rather, the lives of everyone around him. He'd blamed everything on Natasha, spent all that time moaning: how could she do this to me, how could she leave me... But what about him? What was his excuse? Danil was on a drip. And Olga... Oh, he couldn't bear to think about Olga. He stopped to catch his breath. He was blinded by the tears that were welling in his eyes. He had to put her out of his mind, to stop the memories becoming real.

He jumped into the first minibus taxi that came along and ended up in the city centre. More public transport, underground passages, the inconvenience of leftover grey snow that had forgotten how to melt. His route home was circuitous, as though he were deliberately attempting to cover his tracks, like a hare. Ignoring his parents he went straight to his room, shut the door and put a Splean CD on full blast.

Only one notable conversation took place all day. His phone rang again and his whole body tensed up, but this time it was his boss. He took the call indifferently, because he expected it to be about his official dismissal, returning his work record book and other such tedious nonsense.

"Hi!" began Maxim. There was no indication, not even the slightest hint that anything had happened between them. "Have you heard about the crash in Samara?"

He had. When Pavel had arrived home his parents were still horrified by that afternoon's news. They had talked about it in hushed, sympathetic tones, then gone to fetch some potatoes.

Pavel was more shocked by the way Maxim just kept talking, without even pretending to care. After hearing the reports from Samara, which were all over the press, clients had been calling the ARTavia phone lines all day as well as Maxim's private mobile number. All of them panicking. A new wave of general hysteria. They needed another training session, more brainwashing: "You're successful, you have invincible karma, you'll never crash with us!" It was a waste of time trying to appeal to their reason, showering them with leaflets and so on. They didn't simply want to be deceived, they needed it – like a drug, in ever-increasing doses and in direct proportion to the number of aircraft that were crashing around them.

And there were more of them. In just half a day Maxim had taken calls from fourteen prospective clients, all of them desperate to sign up with the only airline offering an absolute guarantee of safety. He didn't have time to fill out all the applications. He didn't have time to prepare his speech for that evening's meeting. Maxim couldn't do it alone. He asked Pavel to return to work. On double pay. There was so much to do...

Pavel listened in silence (Maxim was the one driving the conversation). He was astonished that anyone could have so little self-respect, after everything that had been said earlier. Or maybe it was something else... Maybe he saw himself as a tank that wouldn't stop until it reached its final destination, regardless of the obstacles it encountered along the way. Words simply bounced off his armour like peas and he didn't even notice them, because he knew that he could topple mountains and ride roughshod over anyone who got in his way, and no one would be able to stop him. In that case, you had to envy him.

"Hello? Say something!" Maxim realized Pavel wasn't responding, stopped talking himself, then adopted a more conciliatory tone. "Come on, Pavel... Let's not argue, eh? I can't even remember what it was about! Let's put it all behind us and carry on working together. What do you say? We are family, after all."

So he was going to play the "family" card now, was he? Pavel was incensed. Speaking clearly and precisely, he replied, "Don't you ever say that to me again."

Pavel hung up and collapsed onto his bed, turning the music back up again. Well, I'll be a tank too, he thought. And everything can just bounce off my armour.

The dark blue evening blew through the city. The wind seemed sterile and red lights shimmered in the muddy puddles, which had almost completely melted. It was Saturday. People were hurrying home to their TVs, to their early evening entertainment. The only American wedding limousine in the city drove past, bright with inset lights, like a mini-bar sliding out of a recess in the wall. Heads still turned to watch it pass.

Igor cut a lonely figure, standing on the steps outside a small shop as other people ran in and out. The steps were covered with soggy cardboard. It was so strange. Danil's grandmother's apartment – their default meeting place for the past six months – had been locked up, and they had nowhere else to go. They exchanged greetings and bought a couple of bottles of dark beer.

Igor was his usual excitable, dishevelled self, and as they walked he brought Pavel up to speed on the patient's latest news: his confirmed diagnosis, how long he was supposed to stay in bed, what medicines he had to take, the ban on drinking and when they could visit (once the quarantine had ended). They walked past apartment blocks, past doorways leading to the ant-hills of other people's weekends. Outside one of them a group of young people were listening to music, like they used to in the old days, except now the portable stereo had been replaced by a mobile phone turned up to maximum volume.

Pavel wasn't feeling particularly talkative. They ended up sitting with their beers on a low wall beneath the merciless windows of either a polyclinic or a registry office – some kind of state-run establishment, anyway, as evidenced by the enormous tubs of greenery and the portrait on the wall of what was presumably the boss's office. The three of them sat and looked at one another: Pavel, Igor and the portrait, bleached by the windows and bright as day.

Igor soon ran out of things to say about Danil's convalescence, and since his companion remained silent he decided to change the subject. Unfortunately, it rather backfired.

"How's Olga?" he asked, with a salacious grin.

This time Pavel didn't even try to ignore it. He unleashed all his pent-up anger, making his feelings perfectly clear. Exactly two hours previously Olga had sent one final text message. They hadn't switched the lights on in the apartment at that point and the illuminated columns on his graphic equalizer were rising and falling in the twilight, like an urban planning exercise. Pavel clutched his phone for a while, before eventually making up his mind to read the text after all. Then he deleted it. After all.

They drank their ice-cold beer in silence. Igor was quiet, though not for long. He never really took offence, which was upsetting in its own way: he too was apparently unassailable. As if to prove the point, after about five minutes he carried on as though nothing had happened.

"So, I've been thinking about the ARTavia situation... What's our next move? We should probably..."

"Hang on," interrupted Pavel, not entirely sure he'd understood. "Are you suggesting we simply pick up where we left off?"

They stared at one another for a long time in mutual incomprehension. In the ensuing exchange of fire, Pavel suddenly launched into a sermon.

"You can't keep living like this! Don't you get it? You spend your whole life wrapped up in your stupid fantasies, which are pointless and unrealistic, but the fact is that real people are getting hurt because of them. It's not like playing some online strategy game. Okay, so we distributed all those leaflets and flyers, played at being partisans, and like a fool I went along with it... But you know what? It was all a complete waste of time. ARTavia has twice as many clients now, and not because they didn't believe us, but because... Because it's the kind of game that never ends! Danil's in hospital, and it's basically your fault. That's the real cost of your stories. You need to get a grip, Igor. You're not thirteen any more. Inventing your own world and everything around you, that's no way to live!"

"If you ask me, it's the only way to live," Igor replied calmly. "Do you know which was my favourite book when I was younger? *The Adventures of Huckleberry Finn*. I particularly loved the bit where he and Tom stage the kidnapping of the black slave Jim, who goes round telling everyone about it. It's brilliant! That's the way to do it, to invent your own life. What other choice do we have?"

The portrait regarded them through the bleached window with curiosity. Over the years they'd spent getting to know this face it had attained a kind of wholeness. A completeness. It might sound strange, but the essence of the face was concentrated in the nose. They didn't find it strange, though. It had made an impression on the deepest part of their minds a long time ago.

A freshly washed evening hung over the city. As on any weekend some people – sickening numbers of them – were having fun, basking in friendship and love, whereas others were isolated in their loneliness, drumming their fingers on the radiator and crying into their pillows. The darkness in the apartment was cleft by a houseplant, spiky from lack of water, and diluted by the light from the street lamp that filtered through two panes of laboratory glass; Danil's grandmother had lived here, then Danil himself, but now the clock had stopped and there was no one to change the battery. This apartment had known the warmth of family life, widowhood and wild parties, but these cultural layers were no longer of interest to anyone. Treasured belongings become worthless in no time at all. Meanwhile on the other side of the city the opposite was true: in the sparkle and brilliance of fake crystal, a roomful of people sat shoulder to shoulder and were happy. Maxim had decided to change the way he conducted the meeting that evening; instead of him preaching from the rostrum, they were all taking it in turns to say a few words about themselves. The atmosphere was warm and convivial, if a little heightened from the wine they had drunk, but above all they were relaxed and at ease with one another. And how could anyone criticize them for that?

Pavel strode across courtyards with a clear head and surprising equanimity, forging a path through the snow and blinking back at the lights in the doorways. People poured out of a distant café on the far side of a vacant plot of land. Pavel could make out the bride in a puffy white dress, and seconds later he realized what they were waiting for, as a firework exploded and the sky was divided up into red, green and gold. Everyone was celebrating. The whole city. They weren't mourning yet, because the plane had only just crashed; they wouldn't mourn at all, because so few people had lost their lives.

THE PEOPLE'S BOOK

In the St George Hall of the Great Kremlin Palace, way back in the 1970s (those were the days!) she had received a prestigious award from "dear Leonid Ilyich Brezhnev" himself, along with one of the lingering kisses that were his trademark. "She" was the distinguished Soviet writer Vera Mikhailovna Ilm. Now, twenty years later, she was no longer "distinguished" – merely old. In the shabby offices of the district housing authority one meddlesome secretary yelled to another through the wall, "Hey, Lyuda, can you check if people who've received a State prize are entitled to any benefits?" She glanced at Vera Mikhailovna. "There's a… *lady* here who wants to know."

A deliberate pause before "lady". The little madam had probably been about to call her an "old bag", or something worse. She was looking at her with such disdain. Fascist! thought Vera Mikhailovna. Jerking her chin up, she turned round and walked out.

"What on earth was I thinking, barging in there and humiliating myself by asking for handouts?" she muttered indignantly to herself. Her mouth felt dry and unbearably bitter again, and there was a stabbing pain in her chest. She was eighty years old. It's nothing serious, though, she thought. I'll live. Just to spite you all…

Over the course of her long life Vera Mikhailovna had written a number of worthy, instructive books. It was reputed that Maxim Gorky himself may even have leafed through some of her earlier works. After her epic novel *The Pioneers* was published in the 1960s, she'd had a number of youth groups named after her. They'd even tied a Young Pioneer's red scarf around her not-so-young neck. Pioneers, brave and patriotic, they'd all worshipped her... But now not a living soul cared about her. No one offered to help carry her heavy shopping bags, or to sweep the cobwebs from the high ceilings of her "Stalinist" apartment, as they were called nowadays.

Yes, Vera Mikhailovna lived alone. There was nothing particularly unusual about that – such was the fate of many Soviet (ex) prima donnas. But in their case it was largely due to a succession of abortions and divorces, side-effects of the eternal struggle for success, whereas Vera Mikhailovna... To cut a long story short, she'd never met the right person. She'd never had time for a private life. They'd dedicated their lives to the cause: writing books, building socialism... For all the good it had done.

Socialism was a thing of the past. These days it was getting harder and harder to find the energy to get out of bed in the morning, and she struggled to lift the heavy kettle with her right hand. She was certainly feeling her age.

But Vera Mikhailovna wasn't one to complain. Old habits die hard, and her life still revolved around work. Her daily outings were all that she lived for. Every day, after lunch, she would check that the gas and the water were off and that the windows were all shut. Then she would get dressed and walk over to the mirror, where she would brusquely apply her lipstick. She would put a ballpoint pen and a notebook into her handbag, although she never actually seemed to use them when she got there. (The notebook was the old-fashioned kind issued to delegates; this one had 'XXVII Congress' printed on the cover in gold letters.) But over and above all these little rituals the period prior to her departure was characterized by an intensity of focus, a rush of energy and something akin to adrenalin surging through her old veins. She was like a tiger preparing to pounce. Once her preparations were complete, Vera Mikhailovna would lock the door behind her and set off. You'll be surprised to hear where she was going, after all that fussing and fretting... The market! Yes, an ordinary street market, which had sprung up three blocks away.

Oh, the chaos of those street markets in the 1990s! The ubiquitous flattened cardboard boxes, reduced to a sodden mush and squelching underfoot. Hawkers selling fruit, household cleaning products, Chinese dusters. All of it soaking wet, frozen and forlorn. And so many old people! Some selling, others buying – standing in queues or shuffling round in a big circle, like inmates in a labour camp. Jams, pickles, a few pathetic flowers in a jar... Anything to avoid holding out an empty, upturned palm. And there would always be some old dear wearing the most incongruous pair of brightly coloured, synthetic Chinese trainers. There was something farcical about it all.

Vera Mikhailovna was in her element there. No trace of her former arrogance remained. She would spend hours wandering around the market, talking to the sellers, to the buyers, to anyone and everyone. She bargained and she queued. She argued and she agreed. She laughed and she cried. Muttering to herself, trying not to miss a single word, she would memorize everything that she heard: poignant tales of everyday hardships, grievances, gossip, lines from folk songs, jokes and hate-filled tirades about the "democrap" spewed by the enemy government. As far as Vera Mikhailovna was concerned, the Soviet nation was alive and kicking – it had simply gone underground, like an enormous partisan detachment operating throughout the whole of Russia, and she was writing a book about it. A documentary account. A chronicle of its sufferings, its sorrows and – in spite of everything – its joys. Nothing like the novels she used to write, with their conventional format and narrative plots. As part of an adult education course at the Literary Institute Vera Mikhailovna had read, or rather mastered, a colossal tome – a collection of German folklore from the sixteenth century entitled *The People's Book of Doctor Faust*. It contained hundreds of folk tales and historical details. And now she was working on something similar. Every evening, when she came home from the market, she transferred everything she had heard into a large journal. It was going to be her Chronicle. Her *People's Book* – yes, that was a good name for it! The culmination of her creative odyssey.

The following day saw Vera Mikhailovna back at the market, getting caught up in the maelstrom, feeling like a part of the whole. A couple of policeman in uniform appeared and began patrolling the rows of stalls at a leisurely pace. There was something unpleasantly authoritative about the way they were walking. "We're in charge here!" was the message. "We could send you all packing with a wave of our truncheons, if we felt like it. Or maybe we'll settle for a share of your profits instead..." Vera Mikhailovna (author of the epic novel *The Policemen*), like all the other old women at the market, was filled with a passionate hatred. Just look at them, strutting about like they own the place! Trying to intimidate us... Gestapo bullies. How nice, how simple it must be to live like that, dividing the world into black and white.

They approached one ample old woman who was arranging cans of insecticide on a cardboard box. Lots of them.

"How much are you charging?"

"Eleven roubles."

"How come you have so many?"

"They give them to us at the factory, instead of wages. They're probably trying to kill us all off, the evil bastards! They're the ones who need exterminating!"

"Hear, hear!" the others chimed in.

Moments later, Vera Mikhailovna was delighted to witness the following scene, which took place at a stall set with an array of bottles, jars and boxes containing every conceivable variety of household cleaning product.

Everything was cold and wet. The girl behind the counter was wearing so much make-up it looked like war paint. Effectively, it was.

A wizened old woman in a black coat approached the counter and jabbed a finger at one of the bars of soap. Addressing the seller calmly and matter-of-factly, she remarked, "And it's five roubles here too... To hell with you!"

The girl was stunned. Her mouth fell open rather unattractively, and she stared at the old woman's back as she walked away. Everyone within earshot was shocked too. A large woman in a ludicrous bright yellow quilted coat called after the old woman, "Why have a go at her? It's not her fault!"

Vera Mikhailovna was overjoyed. Her *People's Book* was writing itself!

She always walked home the long way, across the square and around the tram ring. Vera Mikhailovna had never been prone to daydreaming or indecision, preferring to get on with things rather than endlessly procrastinating, so it must have been strange for her to have so much time alone with her thoughts. What did she think about as she walked? She didn't really know... And this September was turning out to be particularly cold and wet.

This time she just walked, without thinking about anything except what she would do when she got home. She would light the gas under the kettle, and the apartment would fill with warmth. She would put on her favourite terry-towelling dressing gown. She would walk over to the table and switch on her enormous old lamp with its green glass shade. She would open her journal and fill another page with writing. It would be warm and comfortable, and everything would be right with the world.

In anticipation of a hot cup of tea, her dressing gown and her warm dog-hair socks she decided to take her time, risking frostbite, even prolonging her walk by taking additional detours through courtyards. Her soul was at peace. Even though she hadn't had anything published since 1986 or been invited to talk at a school since 1990. On that occasion, in a quavering voice, she had read the children one of her old stories, in which a Young Pioneer heroically met his end in a burning cornfield.

"You mean… his pants were on fire?" asked one smart aleck with feigned innocence. The little brat had been sent to the headmaster, of course, but it had ruined her evening. She hadn't been to another school since. Not that she'd been overwhelmed with invitations. Her books were of no interest to anyone any more. Neither was she.

The lift was out of order, as usual, so Vera Mikhailovna had to walk up the stairs, panting and stopping after every few steps to catch her breath.

There were two people on the landing: a man holding a bunch of flowers and her neighbour, a formidable old woman whose late husband had worked at the Moscow City Committee. They had always irritated Vera Mikhailovna, this woman and her husband. On 9 August 1963, a story on page two of *Pravda* had referred to her as a "distinguished Soviet writer"; later that day she'd answered her doorbell to find the two of them standing there, all dressed up in their Sunday best. They'd invited her to their apartment for a cup of tea, so that they could get to know one another better, even though they'd lived on the same floor for ten years. "You're part of our circle now!" It was so long ago that Vera Mikhailovna couldn't remember whether the City Committee man had actually said this, or whether it had merely been written all over his beaming face.

"Here's our Vera Mikhailovna," gushed her neighbour. "Back from the market, empty-handed again..." She trailed off without finishing her sentence.

Silly old bat, thought Vera Mikhailovna. Do you really think I can't afford a loaf of bread? That I hang around the market begging for charity? You know nothing about the creative process!

"Hello! I've been waiting to meet you!" The man with the flowers suddenly bowed.

At first she assumed it was one of the Young Pioneers, all grown up. She found this idea very amusing.

Her second thought was that he was very presentable. Nice clothes: an expensive-looking suit, gold-framed glasses. He seemed very polite, too. But he wasn't an intellectual, definitely not. More like a "businessman", as they were called nowadays. A big shot, too, by the look of it. One of the head honchos.

What did he want? Should she let him in? Alive one minute, dead the next! Vera Mikhailovna felt a mixture of fear and excitement. What did it matter? If he wanted to kill her and ransack her apartment, then so be it. Murdered in her own home while she was still working, still fighting! It would certainly be an appropriate conclusion to her *People's Book*.

"Come in."

Inside the apartment, her guest seemed to suddenly remember the flowers.

"Oh, I'm sorry... These are for you. And here's my card. I've got a business proposition for you."

I dare say you'll be expecting a cup of tea now, thought Vera Mikhailovna. His card had gold writing on it:

vice-president of something or other. Not the Academy of Sciences, naturally.

Meanwhile her guest had started talking. His tone was impassive and he wasted no time getting straight to the point (after all, he was a businessman, a busy man). Apologising repeatedly, he reminded Vera Mikhailovna that she was old, that she had no family, that her pension was a pittance and that ownership of this magnificent apartment would be transferred to the state once she died. Didn't that bother her? Actually, no, it didn't. She'd already given everything to the state anyway. A different state, admittedly, but still...

She didn't understand the exact phrase her guest used, but essentially he was suggesting that they sign some kind of contract, whereby legal ownership of her apartment in the legendary Stalinist skyscraper on Kotelnicheskaya Embankment would be transferred to him in the event of her death. In return she would receive significant monthly payments for as long as she lived (which wouldn't be much longer, he no doubt hoped). A thousand dollars a month! It would pay for all her medicine, and she could get all her groceries delivered too. Why? So she wouldn't have to come home from the market empty-handed!

"Everyone else in your circle is doing it," said the man, apparently feeling the need to justify himself. "You know Tikhonov? He used to be really high up in the Soviet government, Chairman of the Council of Ministers. Well, he's been receiving a very generous allowance from Boris Berezovsky, ever since he signed his dacha over to him..."

Our circle again – ha! Those mercenary bastards! She could remember Tikhonov, but only vaguely. Berezovsky, on the other hand, was notorious. A contemporary Russian Mephistopheles. She'd heard more than enough about him. A fine example to follow!

Her guest kept on talking, and Vera Mikhailovna studied him without really listening. He was a smooth operator, no doubt about it: well-groomed, self-possessed, impeccably dressed... Clearly intelligent. Unscrupulous, too. The kind of man who would wear white gloves to murder people. The kind of man who could be moved to tears by a photograph of his dog, whilst sending thousands of children to the gas chambers. Like Doctor Goebbels. Yes, that was it! She couldn't remember what Hitler's Minister of Propaganda looked like, but this smug face in its gold-rimmed glasses would have fitted perfectly. Well, you'll get what's coming to you, "Doctor Goebbels"!

"You look as though you've come to a decision, Vera Mikhailovna."

"I have, indeed. Get out!"

Her guest may have been expecting her to react like this, but if that were the case he hid it well. Apparently disappointed, he got up to leave.

"Well, it's a pity that we haven't been able to come to an agreement. But you've got my card. Why don't you have a little think about it..."

"Your card is going straight in the bin! I don't want to see you ever again!"

The years fell away, and she felt a rush of joy as she threw him out. Her heart was pounding. She was drunk on her own valour, exhilarated by this heroic deed. For all she knew, it might be her last.

The telephone rang. Damn, the flowers were lying next to it. She should have thrown them in his face!

"Hello, is that Vera Mikhailovna Ilm?"

She gave a start. What now?

"Good evening, this is the director of District Housing Authority 182. I heard that you came in to ask about benefits earlier today. I can confirm that you are entitled to certain benefits. But I gather that you walked out without the information you requested... Why? If you fill out an application form, we can..."

"I don't want anything from you! Leave me alone!"

She slammed the receiver down. Oh, her heart... She could feel that stabbing pain in her chest again. It's nothing serious, though. I'll live. Just to spite you... One shuffling step after another, she reached the table. There was her journal, with its red cover. Her *People's Book*. It was nothing – she, poor old Vera Mikhailovna, would be fine. She would sit at the table and write about the day's events. The new era had burst in on her, catching her off-guard with its new rules, and its representative had been a perfect illustration of the changing times: a modern-day Raskolnikov, armed with a pen instead of an axe. A demon of our time. Had she been tempted? He had tried his best to persuade her to sign the contract, but she would never sell her soul! She had to finish what she'd started, her grim and merciless chronicle of a people betrayed.

Yes, the new era had forced its way in through her door. Once upon a time people had screamed and fainted when they saw the Lumière brothers' legendary cinematic train rushing towards them. Some had even fired guns at the screen. Now it was the new century rushing headlong towards them, every bit as relentless and terrifying, and people were firing at it for all they were worth. Desperate measures, taken in vain.

Vera Mikhailovna Ilm died later that night. The state did indeed take ownership of her apartment, as her guest had foretold, and the district housing authority lost no time in disposing of her personal effects. No one knows for certain what happened to the *People's Book*, but it was never seen again.